Craft

Features

Your Verses

Cover by S
Blouse from
Jacket from
Home Shop
ISBN 0-85

D0295764

Complete
Story
by
SUSAN
SALLIS

CALL IF YOU NEED ME

... But as time passed and the phone
didn't ring, he began to realise that he was
the one who needed her.

BEN ADAMS picked up his mail from the numbered box in the hall and stuffed the four letters into his briefcase to be read later at the office. Three bills and an airmail letter from his sister in the States.

He smiled as he drove his car from the ground-floor garage. Eve was a good correspondent; there would be drawings from his two small nieces, May and Edie, and an enormously scrawled "Hi" from his brother-in-law. He remembered his parents' anxiety when Eve had met and married Bradley Schultz ten years ago. If only they were alive now to see how well it had worked out.

Ben turned the car into the old part of town and nosed into a stable-yard alongside a stone house bearing a brass plate which said: Robert Adams & Son, Interior Designers.

Every day he told himself he must order a new plate, changing his father's name to his own and leaving out the "son." He knew he never would. Just as he would never move the firm into one of the new blocks in the city centre.

His father had bought this house and "set up shop" in 1951. The house itself had had a tenant since his mother's death two years ago, but one day Ben planned to move into the high Georgian rooms with the oriel window overhanging the narrow street.

He went through the outer office, calling a brief good morning to his secretary and draughtsman. In his own office there was a pasteboard layout of a house interior. He looked at it frowningly as he slit open Eve's letter. Something was wrong with it and he couldn't think what.

It was one of Eve's usual letters. She transported him to the low rambling house in New Jersey within commuting distance of New York, yet with its own parochial small-town setting.

The customs he had got used to during his four-week stay with them last year sprang to life again. The school bus honking at the end of the track for Edie and May, the big station wagon without gears or "shifts" as Eve called them, the friendly informal socialising around the barbecue pit, the few smart parties in vast apartments overlooking Central Park, when Brad had introduced Ben to his associates as the man who ran a "real old-fashioned one-man band back in the old country."

Brad worked for a firm of architects employing thousands and planning constructions all over the world. It was how he had met Eve.

And it was at one of these formal receptions that Ben met Maggie.

He skimmed through the letter quickly. Edie had drawn a picture of matchstick children in a swimming pool and the curt caption: *Me swimming, May drowning.* And then, with heart-stopping suddenness, he saw her name. He swallowed and spread the airmail page flat on his desk. After all this time, there was some news.

Do you remember asking me about Maggie Allender? Eve wrote. *Well, guess what? After disappearing off the face of the earth, she came into Brad's office last Tuesday and asked after you.*

Brad told her you were fine and asked her why she didn't write. And she said — mysteriously, I thought — that you were just a phone call away. What does this mean, little brother? Is there something you should tell me? Kindly reply by return.

Ben folded the wafer-thin paper quickly as if he could keep Maggie Allender safe inside. She'd gone into Brad's office . . . just to enquire for him? Of course not. She had worked for Moreno Incorporated, hadn't she? There were lots of people she would want to look up there. Yet she remembered what he'd said about the phone call . . . But she had not phoned. And it was a whole year.

H E sat back in his chair with a feeling of terrible disappointment. Was this her way of letting him know that she did not need him? She must know that Brad would report everything to Eve and that Eve would write to him. So she was telling him something. But what?

He forced himself to recall their few, precious meetings in detail and to feel again that particular magic they had made, to examine it carefully as he would the drawing — or model — of house alterations, in an effort to find a flaw or an oversight.

It had been at one of Brad's stuffy parties, of that he was certain. Names weren't so easy to remember. The senior partner Lucas Moreno and his faded wife. Tertius Knox who ran Constructions Inc., and smoked Churchillian cigars. A bevy of staff with their ladies.

"You must meet Miss Allender, Ben." Brad took his arm and drew him towards another group. "She's on the accountancy side and never brings a partner. You could take her in to dinner."

"Thanks a lot," Ben said, smiling politely through gritted teeth. "I'll remember this, dear brother-in-law."

Brad grinned. "I haven't had my wife to myself for a week without you around. Get yourself a nice friend and go play some place else!"

Brad singled out a small, fair-haired girl in a calf-length chiffon dress, attractive but not stunning, rather solemn looking. She smiled up at Brad as he introduced them. When he had gone, she fished in her shoulder-bag, produced a pair of enormous spectacles and put them on. She looked so like an owl that Ben's polite smile became a broad grin. Immediately her own smile widened to meet it. She gave a small breathless laugh.

"I'm delighted to meet you, Mr Adams."

"Call me Ben. Please, Miss Allender." He meant it. He felt at ease with her immediately.

"Then you must call me Maggie."

They continued to smile at each other.

"You're an accountant, Brad tells me." Ben led her away from the others and picked up a drink from a passing tray. "This is what you are drinking, I think."

"Yes, it is. How did you know?"

"Because it's what I'm drinking, too, and it's the only soft drink except Coke that it's possible to get in this country."

She gave her delightful laugh again and he found he was watching her mouth as it turned up at the corners, her nice, even teeth, the way her eyes closed behind her glasses and opened very wide. They were blue.

MAGGIE was very honest. When he asked her again about her work she shook her head. "I'm not an accountant, Ben, I do bookkeeping and programme a computer to give me a lot of information, costs, salaries and so forth."

He marvelled. "You must be the only ordinary person here. You do realise that everyone else either has letters after their name or is married to someone with letters after their name?"

She nodded solemnly. "I'm one of the masses, Ben. It's very good of you to talk to me."

Even this early in their acquaintance, he could look at her mock sternly and say, "Maggie Allender. Get off your knees."

He thought she was teasing him, but as the evening went on he found that she did have a poor opinion of herself. She said she had no hobbies, and when asked what she did with her spare time she shrugged.

"Well, I do things everyone else does, I guess. I knit and sew and I play some tennis in the summer and swim sometimes and —"

"I thought you had no hobbies?"

"Well, they're not real hobbies, are they? I mean I can't do any of them well. And I'm not crazy about any of them." She looked at him wide-eyed through her spectacles. "I'm not crazy about anything actually," she discovered, horrified.

"If there was a fire in your house . . . apartment . . .?"

"Apartment."

"If there was a fire in your apartment, what would you save?"

"My daughter of course."

Ben was brought up short. "I didn't realise you were married."

"I won't be for much longer. I'm trying to get a divorce."

She did not explain or expand. Because he wanted to keep her with him and because he was unable to ask any personal questions, he told her about his parents and the old Georgian house in the unfashionable quarter of the town where he carried on his father's business.

"Nothing like this of course." He nodded at the others. "We've done the interiors of a couple of churches and a youth club. Mostly houses. Just alterations and extensions."

"Harder to plan, I guess?"

"Not many people realise that."

She looked really interested. "But fascinating. Like cutting up an old dress and making something up to date. Very satisfying."

"Very. Hey, Maggie, what are you doing tomorrow? Eve and Brad want me to go to a builder's congress, but we could have dinner maybe? I've got some drawings with me of our latest conversion. An old tithe barn into a house. Perhaps you'd like to see it?"

He immediately regretted the suggestion. How could he expect a divorced American woman to understand an elderly retired couple wanting to make a home from an ancient, run-down barn?

But she nodded very enthusiastically indeed. She was honest in that way, too, and never made any secret of the fact that she liked Ben.

They met for dinner. He told her about his mother living on in the house after his father's death. Her determination to keep it going as before, her tentative hope that he would one day take it over himself.

She said, "As I told you, Ben, I'm no accountant, but it sounds as though that old place is a drain on the business. Something modern and more central would be more economical. And of course, you wouldn't want to live there, I guess. Your apartment sounds a better bet."

They had been so in tune that he was surprised she could not share his sentimental feelings about the old house.

"What was your home like, Maggie?" he asked. "I mean, when you were a girl."

"We lived in apartments. Always. My father travelled a great deal and when he was going to be some place for longer than a couple of weeks, we usually joined him." She gave her small gurgle of a laugh. "Ma didn't care where we were so long as it was with him."

She told him about some of the schools she'd attended. He began to understand why she hadn't ever qualified in accountancy. There had never been time. For the same reason her friends were few and far between.

"That's how I came to be married," she said wryly at their third meeting. "I thought I'd better do it before we moved on again."

She sighed. "Marry in haste, repent at leisure."

She did not speak of her daughter and he had almost forgotten the child's existence until their fourth meeting.

"I've done most of the tourist things in New York," he said. "Empire State, Statue of Liberty. But I haven't had a buggy ride in Central Park."

THEY were walking down the endless length of Fifth Avenue and the drizzle of rain was increasing by the minute. She stopped and took a telescopic umbrella from the depths of her bag. It was a complicated business to open it and they laughed together as they struggled with the flapping spokes.

"Believe it or not, neither have I," she said breathlessly. "Ridden through Central Park, I mean. And I've lived in New York for four years!"

"Then let's do it. Now."

"Oh, but, Ben . . ." She stopped and looked up at him and there was apology on her round, sweet face. "Oh, Ben, Daisy would love it. Could she . . . tomorrow perhaps . . . would you mind?"

"Daisy?"

"My little girl."

"Ah. Yes. Well, of course, Maggie. Bring her along. Er — how old is she?"

"Five and two months."

His niece, May, had been five and two months last year. What sort of toys had she liked? Had she had much conversation? The trouble was that even now May talked through her big sister, Edie. He couldn't remember having a one-to-one chat with her in the whole month he'd been over here. What in the world would he say to Daisy Allender?

He bought a Victorian doll with frilly petticoats and drawers and button boots. Daisy turned up clutching a pair of skates because after the ride she wanted to go to the skate park. She wore dungarees and a baseball cap and had obviously never held a doll in her life.

She found the ride boring.

"Do you ride a horse and chase foxes back in England, Ben?" she asked seriously. "I'd rather do that, you know, than just sit here and look out at all those trees and grass in the rain."

"I'm afraid I can't ride a horse, Daisy."

"How about a motor cycle? Do you ride a motor cycle?" she asked hopefully.

"No. I drive a car actually."

She wrinkled her tiny nose. "You're like Mother. You don't do anything interesting, do you? My father rides horses. And motor cycles. And he skin-dives. And he's the best skater in the world."

Maggie said nothing; he noticed that she was holding Daisy's hand all the time. Or was Daisy holding hers?

He searched his mind. "I can row. A boat, you know? I used to be in a rowing eight."

She gave him a long look from blue eyes very like her mother's. "Can you water-ski?"

"No." The horse clip-clopped ahead of them, the beauties of the park rolled by, misty with rain, and all he felt was demoralised.

"My father can water-ski," she said. "He does it all the time. He can do almost anything."

Maggie held the doll while Daisy wobbled around the edge of the skate park. She did not try to explain Daisy and she did not mention Daisy's father. Ben was conscious of the cold and damp and wondered whether he had picked up a chill.

After she had called to Daisy that it was time to go home, she turned to Ben.

"It was a beautiful ride, Ben. Thank you for taking us. I'll remember it always." She pulled her small daughter to her, almost squashing the doll, and held her like a shield between herself and Ben. "That was splendid, Daisy — junior skating champion, eh? Now how about some real English tea with Ben? I know a place where we can get muffins."

"I'd rather have milk and cookies back home, Mother," Daisy said, burying her face in Maggie's skirt, not looking at Ben. "Let's go home now, please!"

They made no arrangements to meet again, but he couldn't go back without saying goodbye. He called when Daisy was at school and found Maggie making bread dough in the tiny kitchen.

"I thought you'd buy bread in and get it out of the freezer as you needed it," he said, only half joking. "How come a modern American lady like you with a career and a smart apartment —"

MAGGIE waved floury hands at him. "Don't tease, Ben. I'm moving into a brownstone ground-floor apartment next week. There's a back yard for Daisy with a proper clothes-line for me. I'm going to be a housewife."

She laughed to let him know she wasn't serious and left the bread to take care of itself. They went into a bland, anonymous living-room and drank coffee. There were lots of plants in hand-thrown

Continued on page 20.

Cancel

Everything

**". . . And spend
the day with me,"
he begged.
"For old times' sake."
So she did —
just for
old times' sake.**

THE pianist was playing that lovely old song "I Wish You Love" — and the lounge bar of the Sommers Hotel seemed to be exclusively peopled by couples who looked at each other over the tops of their drinks. They were people who talked with their eyes.

Janice giggled at the scene and took another sip of her drink.

"This is nice," Harry said. "Aren't you glad I found you?"

"Of course," Janice agreed with a smile, and she decided he hadn't changed. He was still a romantic.

**Complete
Story
by
BARBARA
CHAMPION**

He hadn't "found" her, he'd only nearly knocked her flat as she was coming out of the Post Office, she reflected with amusement. Their meeting was purely accidental.

"Olive?" he enquired, pushing a small circular dish towards her. "Crisps, peanuts?" He shuffled the appetisers around, hoping to tempt her with one.

Janice took an olive on a tiny plastic fork.

"Not too many," she said, "or I'll never eat lunch."

The plush hotel bar was one of the smartest in town . . . all concealed lights, rich velvet drapes, cream and gold wallpaper, and maroon carpets so thick that your high heels wobbled as you walked.

HARRY pulled his chair closer to Janice and spoke in confidential tones.

"Why don't we do this again? I've got three more days."

Janice wagged a finger at him.

"Now, you know that isn't possible." She knew her eyes twinkled at him, despite the rebuke.

"Ah, you're still so gorgeous." He sighed. "Why did I ever . . ."

He leaned very close to her left ear and was about to make more of the matter when a polite cough interrupted Harry's train of thought, announcing the arrival of a green-coated waiter.

"Your table for two is ready, sir."

"Thank you, yes, thank you," Harry replied, a little too grandly, Janice thought, suppressing a smile. To the strains of "I'll See You Again" they walked through to the restaurant.

Because Harry had worked abroad for so long, he insisted that they both have the Chef's Special which was simply roast beef with Yorkshire pudding and two veg., followed by apple pie and cream.

"We must have a traditional British meal. I've been looking forward to roast beef for ages," he said, with a boyish grin.

"Well, in that case, we can't disappoint you," she replied quickly.

How he hated his plans to go wrong!

Anyway, even beans on toast would have been a novelty as long as she didn't have to cook it herself.

They talked lightly throughout the meal. And she listened whilst he regaled her with tales of his travels during the past nine years and mentioned the names of many famous towns in the United States.

From time to time he pointed out how much he had missed her, how often he had thought about her.

"But you didn't write," she challenged. "You never sent any postcards."

"Well, one doesn't these days, does one?" He laughed. "Post-cards with 'wish you were here' on the back . . . people just don't do that now."

"Don't they?" Janice asked in an innocent voice.

For a moment he looked at her, a little surprised, then she spoke again. "No, you're probably right."

He smiled then and she thought, as she had so often before, how handsome he was. Tall, broad shouldered, casually dressed, fair hair cut in a trendy style, grey eyes shrewd and aware. He was every bit the man of the moment, and totally different from Brian.

"What *are* the other things you have to do today?" he asked.

Janice ate the apple out of the pie and pushed the pastry aside. She thought of the list in her handbag.

"The chiropodist at two-fifteen, the hairdresser at three o'clock, the library books before five-thirty and a quick call at my mother's place at six," she said, having memorised it all, anyway.

"I can think of several plausible excuses," Harry replied.

"Oh, no, I couldn't." Janice was firm. "Tuesday afternoons are mine. I have a ritual and . . ."

"Break it." He leaned towards her.

"No, no, it's all arranged."

"I've got a pocketful of ten-pence pieces," he said, persuasively. "Let's phone up and cancel everything."

All through the coffee, Janice explained why she couldn't possibly break her appointments, while Harry silently mocked her with his eyes.

As he guided her through the hotel foyer he firmly pulled her off to the right and wedged her into a telephone alcove.

Without speaking, he reached in his pocket and then slapped a handful of small change on the shelf.

Shrugging, Janice took out her diary, phoned the chiropodist and the hairdressers' and cancelled her appointments. She said she'd call again next week.

"I've bumped into an old friend . . ." She explained to her mother. "I'll see you next week as usual."

Harry settled Janice into the front passenger seat of his hire car, and jumped in beside her.

"Now," he said, enthusiastically, "where did we used to go?"

Janice spent several seconds smoothing her skirt.

"Sometimes we went to the pictures . . ." she ventured.

"In the afternoons?"

"Yes, in the afternoons," she said, indignantly. "Sometimes we went prowling around antique shops or markets. And we were some of the first visitors to the bird sanctuary out at Barlow." She thought for a moment, then continued. "We used to walk on the hills, visit the art gallery." At that she stopped and looked at him, accusingly.

"You didn't like the museum. We went jumbling, too . . ."

"I never went to a jumble sale," Harry protested.

"Yes you did, quite often, on Saturday afternoons . . . that's where you picked up that portable radio."

"Ah, yes, I remember it well," Harry said, and they both

CANCEL EVERYTHING

laughed. "But it's Tuesday, so which do we do first?"

"I don't know, but we *must* go to the library at some time." Brian would never forgive her if she forgot his books.

"Well, let's start with Barlow," Harry decided, as he switched on the ignition and coaxed the car into gear.

Harry, as always, was the perfect escort. Kind, thoughtful, attentive and warm, which was just as well because the bird sanctuary was up on the river under a low mist.

They hadn't walked far before Harry ran back to his car and brought her his woollen scarf. He wound it twice around her neck and tied it in a loose knot under her chin.

In between talking to coots, barnacle-geese, swans, mallards and Egyptian ducks, they reflected on the nine years which had passed since they last met.

They spoke of their families, their major and minor dramas, hopes, dreams and, absurdly, the best time of year to plant gladioli.

Around four-thirty they had a proper cream tea in the converted barn adjacent to the sanctuary offices.

"This is the sort of thing I miss," Harry said. "I miss kippers and sausages, red buses, drizzle, fish and chips in newspaper, the BBC, old cars, and you."

"Not me." Janice sighed, deeply.

"Yes, you," Harry insisted.

"No, you never did," Janice insisted, shaking her head slowly.

Harry thought for a moment. "But I will now," he said.

AS they walked to the car, Harry got his drizzle. The day was fading away and the weather had changed.

"Remember we have to change the library books," Janice reminded him.

"All right, let's change the books and keep the peace," Harry agreed.

It was while they were in the library that Harry noticed that Janice's hair had gone straight.

"You've lost your curls," he said.

"It was the mist."

"Suits you," he said decisively.

They were lucky to find the current best seller, a popular thriller and the autobiography of a famous parliamentarian.

"Will these hold the household together?" Harry asked.

"Oh, I think so," Janice replied lightly.

"Let's run away together," Harry suggested suddenly as he helped Janice back into his car.

"Yes, let's," she agreed, her eyes wide.

"We could fly to San Francisco and throw one-penny pieces off The Golden Gate Bridge," he added.

"Wonderful idea. And we could gamble away my mortgage in Las Vegas," she added, wickedly.

"We could open a fish and chip shop on Sunset Boulevard."

"And take a London taxi with us." Janice laughed.

He stopped at the bottom of her street and asked if he could see her again before he went back to the States.

She looked at him for a few seconds and slowly shook her head, hoping her eyes wouldn't twinkle as she was sure they had earlier.

HARRY kissed her soundly and then sent her home. Janice didn't look back.

Before she'd removed her front door key from the lock, Janice called to her husband. "Brian!"

There was a muffled reply from the direction of the kitchen.

Janice followed the sound and found him carefully laying out the salad she'd prepared earlier. The kettle was boiling and the table was laid.

"You're a bit late, aren't you, honey?" Brian enquired.

"Just a bit . . . sorry," Janice replied.

"Never mind, did you have a good day?" he asked.

"Fine, did you?" Janice poured hot water on the tea.

"Same as usual . . . hey!" He spun round. "You've changed your hair!"

Janice patted the limp, straight strands around her face.

"They've done it well, it suits you," Brian added, and walked towards her.

"There's my girl," he said fondly, as he kissed her on the neck. Well, that is he tried to kiss her on the neck.

"Where did you get this awful scarf?" he asked.

Janice had forgotten all about the scarf and as she loosened it she smiled smugly.

"It was a gift," she teased him a little. "A gift from Harry Raglan. You remember Harry Raglan?" She hesitated. "He's home, just for a few days."

17

B

your Verses

LOVE AT THE LIBRARY

Browsing through the
book shelves
Never in a rush,
All the quiet people
Move in silent hush.

Sitting at a table
Both afraid to look,
Suddenly he spies her
Lowering her book.

Eyes meet, both smile
shyly
Fingers softly touch.
Does she come here often?
Dare he ask so much?

The old librarian looks across
He wonders, is it chance,
They're sitting in the section
That's headed —
True Romance!
— **C. H., Treorchy.**

CANCEL EVERYTHING

"Harry Raglan? What, that chap you nearly married?"

"Nearly got engaged to . . . I didn't nearly marry him, darling."

"And a good thing too," Brian stated. "Short chap with a lisp, wasn't he? Not good enough for you, not good enough."

Brian placed the food on the table and went off into the lounge. His nonchalance was beginning to annoy her.

"Sit down, relax," he called over his shoulder. "I'll just change into my slippers."

"I had to cancel some appointments today," she began.

"Ah, too bad," Brian said as he came back into the kitchen and joined her at the table.

"We went to the bird sanctuary," she said, stirring her tea, but watching her husband's expression.

"Very nice too," he replied. "You should get as much fresh air as you can."

She was going to get very angry soon.

"Before that we had lunch at the Sommers and . . .."

"The Sommers! Good Lord, come into money, has he?" Brian laughed.

"We also had tea out so I'm not really that hungry." She tried to make the tone flippant.

"Well, eat what you can."

Janice tapped the table with the handle of her fork, impatiently.

"Brian," she said, with barely controlled patience, "I'm trying to

MINIATURES

All the little memories
  Are dustings of pure gold
That sprinkle like a blessing
  On the shades of growing
    old.

It's not the most momentous,
  But just the little things
That gently coax a smile
    from me
  And give my thoughts
    their wings.

Basking in the sunshine,
  Walking in the rain,
Dancing in the moonlight
To "our own" refrain.

Holding hands and dreaming,
  Confidences shared,
Whispering sweet nothings
  Just to show we cared.

Mown grass in the springtime
  Burnt leaves in the fall,
Cosy winter firelight —
  Perhaps the best of all.

The days my arms first held
    you
Are a long time in the
    past —
But while my heart is
    beating
My love for you will last.
     — **V. R., Shrewsbury.**

CANCEL EVERYTHING

tell you something I think is important."

"I know you are," he replied. "You are trying to tell me that you cast aside all that's dear to you, all your obligations, and went trotting around town and country with your old flame . . ."

"Well, it wasn't quite like . . ." This wasn't the reaction she'd expected.

"An old flame, I might add, who was branded as 'boring' nine years ago and henceforth banished to one of our ex-colonies," he stated blandly.

"He wasn't short with a lisp," Janice burst out.

"I know, I know, he was tall, fair and perfect. I remember Harry Raglan very well if I want to, and I don't want to, all right?"

Janice sighed and pretended to look miserable.

"I just wanted you to know how much I love you, darling," she explained.

"Fine, that's great." Brian put down his knife and fork. "Now, let me ask you something important."

"Yes?" Janice said, quietly.

"In all this wining and dining at five-star hotels . . . did you manage to change the library books?"

She laughed, happily.

"Yes, of course I did."

"Then, in that case . . ." Brian paused. "I love you, too." He patted the back of her hand. "Now, eat your salad," he said. □

CALL IF YOU NEED ME

Continued from page 11.

pots and a hooked rug, and sitting in an armchair, obviously discarded, was his doll.

"Look, I'm sorry about yesterday," he said awkwardly. "Daisy was bored stiff."

Maggie smiled. "I don't think so. She was cautious. Testing you out."

"And finding me wanting."

"I don't think so, Ben. She's just scared of men."

He remembered Daisy in her cap and dungarees, so different from Edie and May it was incredible. But, of course, Maggie had to protect the child. He understood suddenly why there was never an escort for Maggie when she went out. There was no room in her life for anyone except Daisy. Ben himself had been an ideal companion because his visit was so short.

He said, with a sinking heart, "It's been marvellous meeting you, Maggie. If you're ever in England —"

She laughed, but it wasn't her usual happy sound. "I'll call you. Don't worry."

"Yes. Yes, do that. In fact . . . if you ever need me, call. I'm just a telephone dial away, remember. Will you do that?"

She was silent and he thought she might be going to tell him she needed him right then. But at last she nodded briefly.

"Yes. I'll remember that. And you remember it, too, will you?"

"Of course. Of course I will."

Ben frowned now as he remembered the bleakness of his flight home, then the waiting and the hoping for the phone to ring. She had never called.

He had written to her at the apartment and the letter came back to him after three long months with a pencil scrawl across it: "Gone away." It was ridiculous, surely she would have left a forwarding address. If she'd moved, there wasn't much point in trying to phone her. Unless she had gone back to her husband, of course. He tortured himself with thoughts of them horse-riding and water-skiing.

He mentioned her casually in his next letter to Eve. Eve replied that Maggie Allender had left Moreno Inc. quite soon after his return to England. Brad had asked the girls in Accounts about her but they knew nothing.

Finally he had decided there was nothing more he could do. He tried to forget her.

His secretary, Sylvia, came in with the letters and they went through them quickly.

She paused on her way out and looked at the pasteboard model. "You know what's wrong with that, don't you?" she asked.

She had worked for his father and treated him as if he was still a teenager.

"I know you don't care for the circular hall, Sylvia," Ben said absently, his mind still in New York. "But it's a feature of the place and — "

"It's not that. Though why anyone should want it, I can't think. Carpets will be tricky, and there'll be no handy corners for coat hooks. But it's not that. The bathroom should be where the kitchen is. And the kitchen should be where the bathroom is. You've got it back to front."

BEN looked. She was right! How could he have been so blind? Had he been too close to the project for too long?

And quite suddenly he saw something else, too. He had another thing back to front. He had expected a shy, inhibited woman, who had probably sworn never to be "hasty" again, to telephone him. To get in touch with a man she had known for a brief three weeks and who lived in a foreign country in a manner completely different from anything she had known.

He smiled widely. "Thank you, Sylvia. Thank you very much indeed. You're a genius."

She looked surprised. "You would have seen it yourself soon, Ben. It's so obvious."

He laughed delightedly. Then sobered. Even though he had at long last "seen it for himself," what could he do about it? Maggie had moved from the apartment. Daisy did not like him. The problems were not going to disappear.

Again he sat down while he thought about it. She had gone in to see Brad deliberately, he was sure of that now. And she had reminded Brad — reminded Ben really — that she was just a phone call away. Even if she had moved she might have kept the same phone number.

He lifted the receiver, impatient with himself. The number was long but indelibly imprinted on his mind. He could dial direct.

It rang and rang. When he was about to give up there was a click and a voice said thickly, "Hello — hello — who is that, please?"

Ben felt happiness fizz through him; it was Maggie's voice.

"It's all right," he said. "It's me, Ben. I've just read Eve's letter and I realise that I must be the one to call you, so I'm calling."

There was another long pause. Then she said, "I've just switched on the light. Do you realise it's four in the morning?"

He said. "Oh, lord. No, I didn't think. I just had to ring to tell you I love you. I'm sorry, darling. I just didn't think."

A gurgle of a laugh reached his ears. He knew suddenly that whatever the difficulties, her mood was the same as his. She was happy.

"Ben, don't be sorry. If you mean that . . . what you said . . . I don't care what time it is. Oh, Ben."

"Darling, I would have told you straightaway, but when Daisy went on and on about what a superman her father is, and when I thought you were happier without a permanent home . . . oh, I don't know."

"Ben, I've never *had* a home, not a settled home. But that doesn't matter anyway. I'm like my mother, home is where you are. Anyway, listen. I took that apartment in the old brownstone, remember? And Daisy just loves the back yard, and so do I. And I went back to school to get some qualifications and I've got them now so I can work shorter hours and go on making a home for us — "

"Are you telling me you don't need me?" he asked.

"No, Ben. I'm just telling you that I can make a marvellous home in an old house. And Daisy would love it. And you could be proud of me because I've got letters after my name. That's all."

"But you're back at the apartment now. The phone number — "

"I took my phone number with me. In case you called." Her voice was small and apologetic.

He laughed again. "Oh, Maggie, I do love you." He remembered wryly his hours of hard thinking. "I thought you'd gone back to superman. Water-skiing. Horse-riding."

"Ben, you don't understand, do you? Bob couldn't do any of those things. He never visits Daisy, she doesn't remember him. But she wants a father badly. The doll you gave her is called Vicky and always sits in the best chair. And when we go to the park Daisy wants to take a boat out. You were the first man I took her to meet, so she was very nervous."

He took a deep breath. "Tell her I'm coming over. As soon as I can get a flight. Tell her maybe we could learn to water-ski together. Tell her I'll teach her to row if she'll teach me to skate. Tell her — "

She spoke very softly into the phone. "I'll tell her, you're just a call away, Ben. And if she shouts silently, like I did, you'll always hear."

He digested this. Then he said the only thing there was to say.

"I love you." □

OUR QUICK CROSSWORD

Sit back, relax — and test your wits with our crafty crossword.

ACROSS

1. Began a game of cards (5)
4. You're wrong to believe it? (6)
8. Desert greenery (5)
9. Mild — but with anger consumed! (9)
11. A spread by the fireside (6-3)
12. Friends changing teams (5)
13. Deadly spider (9)
16. Bandaged and recorded? (5)
18. Merry lady of operetta (5)
19. Sherlock's method (9)
21. Distress if Reg goes astray (5)
23. They turn to guns (9)
26. Distributors of hot air! (9)
27. Red-faced because of it? (5)
28. Old-fashioned golf-club (6)
29. They're apart through over-eating? (5)

DOWN

1. Gave up hope (9)
2. It's in your favour (5)
3. Someone teaching about trout? (5)
4. Dad's Army (4, 5)
5. Having pains jointly? (9)
6. Don't go straight! (5)
7. Path to altering headwear? (3-3)
10. Brought relief (5)
14. Lightning information? (4-5)
15. Rare in a restaurant? (9)
17. Snips of bargains? (5-4)
18. Move about royalty having a bet? (5)
20. Made a home for young birds (6)
22. Revising aid in part of Asia (5)
24. Ornaments in Eva's estate (5)
25. Girl turning to Ronald endlessly (5)

Solutions On Page 94.

23

Complete Story by SHEILA LEWIS

THE ear-splitting crash of shattering glass penetrated the air. Graham Anderson looked up from the book he was reading. Upper gymnasium, he thought, without anger or concern, just an apathetic acceptance.

He didn't feel like dealing with it today, or any day for that matter. He just longed for the time when he'd be away from all this. Away in the country, out of sight and sound of people.

He had decided that he could take no more. He simply must put his house on the market, must send in his resignation to the Education Authority, must decide which to do first.

There was a peremptory knock on the door. He knew that it heralded his deputy, Miss Proudfoot. She swept in, quivering with

"Please, Sir, It's Jones, Sir!"

Of course it was Jones! If there was a mouse in the dining-hall, a broken window in the gymnasium, a fight in the playground — who else would it be?

anger and frustration, not even waiting for Graham's invitation.

"I expect you heard that crash, Headmaster. That boy again, a football again, the upper gymnasium. Last week it was the field-mouse in the school canteen — the week before, the history books turned up in the botany shed. You *will* be doing something about him this time!"

It wasn't a question. It was a command.

"Yes, Miss Proudfoot," he said wearily. "I will."

Anything to make her go away.

"Send him in. And ask the janitor to send for the glazier."

With an audible click of her tongue, Miss Proudfoot departed.

Graham got up from his desk and walked over to the window. His room was at right angles to the gymnasium block and he could see the jagged remains of the window which the janitor was already knocking out with a hammer.

Some fragments of glass littered the flower beds under the gymnasium windows. Graham reflected that the architect of the school had known what he was about. Had there been no flower bed, the glass might have fallen straight on to the playground.

He heard another knock on his door.

"Come in," he said without turning round.

There was a scuffle of footsteps, the door closed and a small voice spoke: "Please, Sir, it's Jones, Sir."

Graham closed his eyes. He might have known. It was *always* Jones. Everyone in the school knew Jones was responsible for the mouse and the mysterious transportation of the history books, but he hadn't actually been caught. But this time . . .

"How did you come to break the window, Jones?"

"Not my fault, Sir. No really, not just an excuse. It was Wheeler. He's a useless goalkeeper. Couldn't save a feather from the wind. I got this ball, see, and it was a fantastic right cross, you should have seen it, Sir." The boy's voice took on a lyrical quality.

"It sort of soared, angle was right, just going in the corner of the net. Wheeler should've saved it," he finished self-righteously.

Graham turned round from the window.

"I take it the corner of the net was the upper gymnasium?"

Jones thought on his feet, where football was concerned at least.

"Wind took it, Sir. Right up." His look of innocence was marred by the black eye he was sporting.

The wide, generous mouth, slightly shadowed with mud, was risking a smile.

"Does Wheeler have india-rubber in his shoes?"

"Goalies are meant to jump, Sir," Jones protested. "You've told us that. Nobody is any good since you stopped taking the team. When you going to start it up again? It's three months since — "

Graham thumped his fist on the desk. "Do you know how much that window will cost to replace?"

Immediately, he could have bitten out his tongue.

Jones blanched and the wide mouth fell. "N-no, Sir."

Graham could read the worry in the child's mind. There was no money in the Jones home for anything extra. Mrs Jones took cleaning jobs where and when she could.

Mr Jones had left town quite suddenly four years ago. She'd never received any word from him, nor any money. No-one could find him to order him to pay his wife maintenance.

Graham was angry with himself. He'd only wanted to stop the boy going on about the football team. However, he was still left with the problem of Jones's bad behaviour.

"Come on, Jones. Let's go and inspect the damage."

Meekly, the boy followed Graham out into the playground.

"I'll tidy it all up, Sir." He bent eagerly to grasp the broken glass.

"No, Jones, you'll cut yourself. Leave that for the janitor. But just look at the damage. Even some of the roses are ruined."

"Roses?"

"The flowers, Jones."

"Oh, them red and yellow things with the prickles on the stalks."

It was on the tip of Graham's tongue to correct the boy's grammar, then he looked closely at him. Jones obviously didn't know much about gardens. And then Graham had an idea.

"Jones, for punishment, you will tidy up this garden. Take away all the dead flowers and broken stems. Then dig. Perhaps all the energy and force that is in your right foot can be directed on to a spade."

"Me? You're not serious, Sir."

"And when you've finished here, I know some old people who need help with their gardens. I can't force you to do them, but I would be very pleased if you would."

"Aw, Sir!"

"After school, Jones. Starting today."

Graham went back to his room, glad to have rid himself of that problem. Detention and extra lessons were no use. Jones had this boundless, volatile energy. There would always be boys like him.

In fact, there was invariably a Jones in every year at school. This was Jones's last year at Thornlet Primary School, and mine, too, thought Graham.

He was sorry he'd shouted at him about the cost of the window. It had been that remark about the football team that had caught him in the raw. He didn't want reminding that he hadn't taken the team since Susie died.

He had enough reminders of Susie — that's why he had to get away. Away from anything that brought back memories. Away from the house, from the school, from people.

He had to do it as much for everyone else's sake as his own. He couldn't run a school in this detached way. The football team was a good example of how he was letting the boys down, in fact the whole school, down.

"PLEASE, SIR, IT'S JONES, SIR!"

JONES met him at the school gate next morning. "Finished, Sir. Like to inspect?"

Graham looked in surprise at the flower bed. Every inch was turned over. The surviving roses looked frail and uncertain amid huge lumps of earth.

"M'mm," he said.

The child had done all this after school yesterday? What energy. It occurred to him that there was still all today's energy stored up inside Jones, too. Heaven knows what mischief that would cause.

"Well dug, Jones, but you can't leave it like that. Rake it over, even it off."

He left Jones looking stricken and muttering, "What's a rake?"

Graham didn't enlighten him but let him find out himself.

The garden was raked during his lunch-break.

"Ready to start on the old folks' garden now," Jones told him as he was leaving school.

That night, Graham called on the Dobsons, who lived two doors away from him. Mrs Dobson looked surprised to see him. In fact, he realised, surprise outweighed the welcome in her expressive face. He could understand that. The neighbours had rallied round with help and comfort after Susie had died, but he'd firmly rejected everyone. He didn't need help and how could anyone comfort him? His life ended with Susie.

Mrs Dobson took him into the sitting-room. Mr Dobson was sitting close to the fire; it was a bad time for his arthritis. Graham realised the old couple were wary, no doubt anticipating another rebuff.

He explained quickly about Jones. "He can dig, I've proof of that, and I'm sure that would be a help to you. He could cut the grass, too. It would take some of the burden off you, Mr Dobson. You'll be doing the school a service, too," he finished wryly.

"That would be a grand help, Mr Anderson. With the weeds growing so quickly, there is a lot to do. I expect Mrs Brown wouldn't mind if he did a couple of hours' work in her garden," Mrs Dobson told Graham.

"Good. Spread the word," Graham said. "Hard work is what the boy needs for a bit."

It wasn't until Miss Proudfoot mentioned it to him that he realised over two weeks had gone past without Jones causing havoc in the school. The same day, the lady living in the end house in Cresswell Crescent, a complete stranger to him, called to him as he passed.

"That's a grand lad you brought us, Mr Anderson. Gardens are going to be a picture this year."

"Ah, yes," Graham said vaguely, his eyes roving over another immaculate flower border. "He's an energetic lad."

He walked up the crescent slowly, looking around in amazement. Every garden bore evidence of being freshly dug. Perhaps he'd solved the problem of troublemakers at school. Ah, well, he could pass on the solution to his successor. It wouldn't be long now. He'd gone straight to the estate agent from school and discussed a selling price for the house.

Graham let himself into the house and decided he'd better take some kind of inventory of the contents. If he planned to take a small cottage, two-thirds of this furniture would have to go. It was a pity really, Susie had had such fun collecting it all. Still, it would only serve to remind him of her constantly. He just couldn't bear that.

He fetched a notebook and pencil and began to itemise the furniture. He didn't get on very fast.

Every single item had its own particular memory, such as the candlesticks she'd bought from a junk yard and when cleaned proved to be solid brass. Or the armchairs she'd re-covered herself, not terribly successfully, after attending the upholstery night class.

As he noted each item, Graham kept hearing her voice and seeing her face.

Suddenly, he flung the book from him. He'd have to do it another day. He leant his hands on the window sill and looked out, unseeing, over the garden. Slowly his focus returned and he was aware that there was movement in the garden — Susie's garden.

He flung up the window and leaned out.

"Hey, you there, what do you think you're doing!"

"It's me, Sir. Jones."

"Wait there," Graham commanded.

He went outside. Jones was standing by the long rose garden, a trowel in his hand.

"Your garden, Mr Anderson, it needs some attention. Look at all them weeds, choke the flowers they will," Jones remonstrated.

"Leave them alone. I don't want this garden touched." Graham knew he sounded unreasonable, but this was Susie's garden, tended by herself. No-one else would be allowed to touch it.

Jones looked at him, puzzled. "I was going to take some cuttings for the school. Mr Dobson showed me how. We need to plant some more flowers where the gym window fell on them. The janitor told me your wife had put the roses there and I thought —"

"PLEASE, SIR, IT'S JONES, SIR!"

"No, Jones." Graham knew that his tone was sharp.

The boy looked at him for a moment and Graham saw the hurt in those vivid eyes.

"I'll look after my own garden, Jones."

"Things die if they're not cared for, Sir," the boy said hesitantly. "Don't you want —"

But Graham was already walking back into the house.

TWO days later, a delighted Mr Dobson called to thank Graham for sending Jones to help.

"He's a grand chap, has a real feeling for growing things. Picks up facts like magic."

Graham smiled, thinking of Jones's abysmal results at school. Maybe the whole idea had a two-fold benefit — for the old people; and a future for Jones.

"Mind you, we'll all be sorry to lose him, but I expect he's paid off the window by now."

"Paid off?"

"We know it started off as a punishment, but the lad has done so much we've all been giving him a little something to help pay for the window. Oh, he didn't want to take it, not from any of us, but he really deserved it."

Next day, Graham called Jones into his room and asked for a complete explanation.

"I've got the money, all of it. I ain't spent any of it."

"Haven't spent any of it," Graham corrected automatically. "But the point is why have you kept it? What do you intend to do with it?"

Jones shuffled and his face got redder.

"I was going to give it to you, Sir, but not yet . . . I like doing the gardens. If I was to give you the money, I couldn't do them no more." His voice went on faster and faster as if to stop Graham telling him that the punishment was over.

"And some of them was in a terrible state, you know, like yours, Sir. Neglected something awful. I like to see things grow. Dug up my own back green last week. I didn't like it much. But I will when I've made a patch and planted bulbs for the spring."

Graham walked to the window while Jones was speaking. Inevitably his gaze fell on the little strip of garden under the gymnasium windows. For the first time he remembered Susie's words when she'd first seen it.

"Look at that strip over there. It's a disgrace. It's neglected. That should never be allowed to happen to a garden, Graham. Nor to a school or to people."

Susie had been delighted when they'd moved to Thornlet and thrilled that Graham had his own school. This is our school, Susie had told him. He had worked so hard and become successful with everything. What would she think if she could see things today?

30

"PLEASE, SIR, IT'S JONES, SIR!"

Graham turned away from the window and faced Jones.

"The insurance company will pay for the window, Jones, and you can put that money to good use. You can buy some plants and cultivate the garden under the gym windows."

The boy's face lit up. "Really, Sir? It'll be the best school garden you've ever seen. Honest. I'll make it just as good as Mrs Anderson had it — " He stopped, drawing his breath, and staring at Graham.

Graham smiled at him. "Yes, Jones, she'd like that. So you'd better take some cuttings from my wife's garden to start you off."

"You bet."

"And you might as well tidy up my garden while you're at it."

Jones nearly smirked.

"Right, Jones," Graham said seriously. "I expect this to be the last time we meet in my room. Understand?"

"You won't see me here again, Sir," Jones said fervently.

When he got home that evening, Graham rang the estate agents and cancelled the proposed sale of the house. He went round every room looking and remembering, this time without the acute pain, just the joy of recalling incidents. How near he had come to betraying Susie by abandoning all that had been so dear to her.

He knew there would be bad times again, but there was something to live for, and people to care for. There was the football team to train for a start.

Football was now banned in the school playground, not by Graham or any of the teachers, but by Jones. No-one dared face his wrath if one of his precious shoots should be damaged.

Peace reigned, but Graham knew it wouldn't be long before some other tearaway came up through the school. Still, he had dealt so successfully with Jones that he felt almost smug about future culprits. He'd soon sort them out.

The euphoria over his success was still with him a few days later when one of the new teachers, Mrs Martin, came into his office.

"Mr Anderson, we've had a spot of bother in the dinner-room today. This boy tipped up the custard dish 'to see if it was as thick as the usual cement,' his expression I may say, and it ran all over the floor. There's a veritable yellow sea of it. He says it was an accident — "

"I've heard that before. Don't worry, Mrs Martin, I'll deal with him. After I've spoken to him we'll have no more trouble. Send him in."

Graham walked over to his window and looked down at the immaculate little garden. It and the gardens in Cresswell Crescent were a living tribute to his ingenuity. They scarcely needed an hour's work a week. Now what could he devise as a suitable punishment for today's offender?

There was a brief knock on his door and he heard the scuffle of feet as the boy entered. The voice was low and apologetic.

"Please, Sir, it's Jones, Sir." □

Complete Story by SARAH BURKHILL

This was her
daughter's day,
but the mother
of the bride
had something
of her own to
celebrate . . .

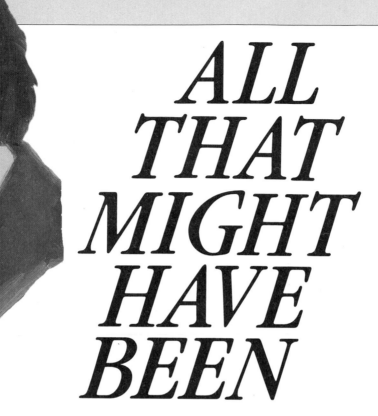

ALL THAT MIGHT HAVE BEEN

THE church is getting quite full now, Jenny. Of course, not all the people here are invited guests. There are some faces at the back that I don't recognise. Women in ordinary, everyday clothing, who were perhaps just passing by and decided to pop in and watch the ceremony.

It's funny how no-one can resist a wedding — especially in this day and age, when marriage is no longer considered the "in" thing, and so many scoff at the vows taken.

But there is something about a bride that makes everyone stop and think. Even me, Jenny, though up until now there has been little time for thought, what with the bustle of preparation and all the last-minute details needing attention.

Now it is quiet, and I am alone, waiting. I suppose this is the time when most mothers think back over the years — to the baby they held in their arms, to its first words, the first stumbling, bumbling attempts to walk. And then to that other parting, the first of many, when school begins and the child that has been theirs alone becomes part of a wider world.

It's fifteen years since you went to school. Fifteen years! In one way it seems such a short time. And yet in another it could be a century ago, a different lifetime.

ALL THAT MIGHT HAVE BEEN

How abandoned I felt then, Jenny, when you raced up the path without even turning to wave, and I went home alone to an empty house. Some women — your Aunt Audrey, for instance — feel a tremendous sense of release when their children go off to school. Suddenly their days are their own, they have no ties, they are free.

But free to do what, I found myself wondering before the first month was out. Oh, I would go into town some days, look at the shop windows, have coffee and cake in a nice little tea-room. And I could go visiting, discuss new teaching methods with the other mothers. But it all seemed so — futile, I suppose, is the word.

"If you feel like that, Susan, why don't you get a job?" your father said, looking up briefly from the papers he was working on. "Give you something to do with your time."

Something to do with my time. Once, years ago it seemed, I hadn't looked on time as a thing to be got rid of, passed in whatever way possible. But now . . .

"Maybe you're right," I told him, and immediately started scouring the situations-vacant column of the newspapers.

It was the following Thursday when I found myself at the offices of Laurence Gray, Estate Agent, trying hard to present a façade of calm and efficiency to this solid, respectable-looking firm.

Mr Gray himself wasn't there, and it was a kindly, grey-haired lady called Pat Owen who interviewed me. The job was simplicity itself, she explained. Just a little typing, answering the phone; later, maybe, occasionally showing clients round houses if Mr Gray were busy.

Did I think it would suit? As she was leaving at the end of the month, and the only other employee was a junior, they were anxious to get someone started as soon as possible.

Was Monday soon enough? I asked. It was, and I spent the rest of the week in a flurry of anxiety over the new rôle I was taking on. Eight years had passed since I'd last worked. What if I couldn't cope? What if Mr Gray didn't approve of Pat Owen's choice? What if he thought I was too inexperienced? What if he thought I was the wrong age, or type of person, or — or something?

My new boss didn't appear in the office on Monday, and it was the next day before I had the chance to learn what he thought about anything at all.

"Hi, I'm Laurie," he announced, bouncing in and scattering files in every direction.

He grabbed my hand in the passing, shook it vigorously, then stopped and peered closer at me, frowning.

"Hey, d'you know you've got green eyes? *Really* green, I mean. You don't often see that. Unusual. Nice, too," he added, giving me a wave as he disappeared into his own little office.

I must have looked as taken aback as I felt, for Mrs Owen gave an exasperated smile and shook her head.

"Don't worry, dear. He's crazy, but you'll get used to it," she said. She didn't bother to lower her voice any, I noticed.

"I heard that, Pat Owen!" Laurie called back, and the older woman just shook her head again and laughed.

MAYBE that little exchange wouldn't seem odd to you now, Jenny, when friendly informality can be so much a part of working life. But at the time I'd last had a job things were different, and I didn't know quite what to make of my casual, crazy employer, and the easy attitudes of that small office.

I didn't see Laurie again until lunch-time. Pat and Cathy, the junior, had already left, and I was on the point of doing so myself when he came out of his room.

"Where do you go for lunch?" he asked.

"Well, I — that is, yesterday I went to that restaurant on the corner," I told him. "It seemed quite nice, so I thought —"

"*Nice?*" Laurie screwed up his face. "Yes, I suppose so, if you're eighty-five. You never see anyone under eighty-five in that place.

"No —" he grabbed my jacket and slung it round my shoulders " — come to the *Rose and Crown* with me. They do a rather excellent cheese toastie. Or cheese and ham.

"Or even —" he was manoeuvring me out the door and along the street "— if you're feeling madly adventurous, cheese and *pickle!*"

And so that's how I found myself perched on a bar stool, with a cheese and onion toasted sandwich and a half pint of cider, listening to this strange young man as he held forth on every subject under the sun.

And do you know something, Jenny? I *enjoyed* it! I really enjoyed it!

I suppose it was odd in a way that I should have thought of Laurie as *young*, for he was the same age as I was and I didn't see myself as young. Perhaps that was the trouble, why I had taken a job in the first place. There I was, 32 years old, growing towards middle-age, and life just seemed to be passing me by.

I know that sounds a cliché, but it's true, darling.

I had never noticed it before, hadn't stopped to think what I might be missing.

But then, I had done nothing but attend to you and your dad. Now you no longer needed me as you once had. And your father — I didn't know about him. Our life together seemed to have become more habit than anything else. Jim had his work, which was difficult and time-consuming. I knew I had you and our home.

But what did Jim and I have together?

We no longer seemed to have anything — not even the joy of shared thoughts, because Jim was a quiet man and used words as if each one were precious, not to be wasted.

Not like Laurie Gray. Laurie talked incessantly, and after the first couple of weeks, I felt I knew everything about him.

Continued on page 38.

# TABLE

Materials Required — Of **Twilleys Stalite**, 1 x 50 gram ball. 3.50 mm crochet hook.

The quantity of yarn stated is based on average requirements and is therefore approximate.

For best results it is essential to use the recommended yarn.

Measurement — 40 centimetres, *16 inches,* in diameter.

Tension — First 8 rounds measure 10 centimetres, *4 inches,* using 3.50 mm crochet hook.

If your tension is too tight, try a size larger hook. If it is too loose, try a size smaller.

Abbreviations — **Ch** — chain; **dc** — double crochet; **tr** — treble; **sl-st** — slip-stitch; **ch-sp** — chain-space.

Note — Figures in square brackets [ ] are worked the number of times stated.

TO MAKE

Make 4 ch, then sl-st to first ch to form a ring.

1st round — Work 8 dc into ring, **do not** join with a sl-st at end of this or next three rounds.

2nd round — Work 2 dc into each dc — 16 dc.

3rd round — 2 dc into first dc, *1 dc into next dc, 2 dc into next dc; repeat from *, ending 1 dc into last dc — 24 dc.

4th round — 2 dc into first dc, *1 dc into next 2 dc, 2 dc into next dc; repeat from *, ending 1 dc into each of last 2 dc — 32 dc.

5th round — 1 dc into each dc, sl-st to first dc.

6th round — 1 ch as first dc, 1 dc into each dc, sl-st to first ch.

7th round — 1 ch as first dc, 1 ch, *1 dc into next dc, 1 ch; repeat from * to end, sl-st to first ch.

8th round — Sl-st into first ch-sp, 4 ch, 1 tr into same ch-sp, *[1 ch, 1 tr into next ch-sp] 3 times, 1 ch, [1 tr, 1 ch, 1 tr] into next ch-sp; repeat from *, ending [1 ch, 1 tr into next ch-sp] 3 times, 1 ch, sl-st to 3rd of 4 ch.

9th round — Sl-st into first ch-sp, 4 ch, *1 tr into next ch-sp, 1 ch; repeat from * to end, sl-st to 3rd of 4 ch.

10th round — Sl-st into first ch-sp, 5 ch, *1 tr into next ch-sp, 2 ch; repeat from * to end, sl-st to 3rd of 5 ch.

11th round — Sl-st into first ch-sp, 3 ch, 2 tr into same ch-sp, *3 ch, miss next ch-sp, 3 tr into next ch-sp; repeat from *, ending 3 ch, sl-st to top of 3 ch.

12th round — Sl-st over 2 tr and into ch-sp, 3 ch, 2 tr into same ch-sp, *5 ch, 3 tr into next ch-sp; repeat from *, ending 5 ch, sl-st to top of 3 ch.

TOPPER

13th round — As 12th round.

14th round — Sl-st to next tr, 1 ch as 1 dc, *7 ch, miss next tr and next 2 ch, 1 dc into next ch, 7 ch, miss next 2 ch and next tr, 1 dc into next tr; repeat from *, ending 7 ch, miss next tr and next 2 ch, 1 dc into next ch, 7 ch, sl-st to first ch.

15th round — Sl-st over next 3 ch, 1 dc into next ch, *7 ch, miss next 3 ch and 1 dc and 3 ch, 1 dc into next ch; repeat from *, ending 7 ch, sl-st to first dc.

16th round — Sl-st over next 3 ch, 1 dc into next ch, *9 ch, miss next 3 ch and 1 dc and 3 ch, 1 dc into next ch; repeat from *, ending 9 ch, sl-st to first dc.

17th round — Sl-st over next 4 ch, 1 dc into next ch, *9 ch, 1 dc into 5th ch from hook (a picot formed), 4 ch, miss next 4 ch and 1 dc and 4 ch, 1 dc into next ch; repeat from *, ending 9 ch, 1 dc into 5th ch from hook, 4 ch, sl-st to first dc. Fasten off.

Press work lightly on wrong side with a warm iron over a damp cloth. □

Our crocheted centre will look charming on your coffee table.

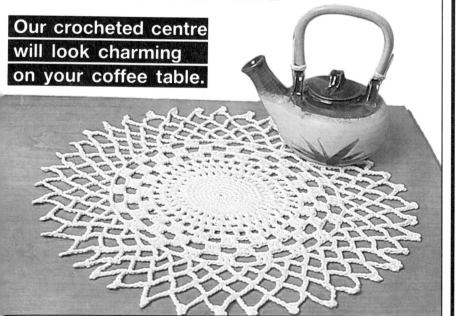

ALL THAT MIGHT HAVE BEEN
Continued from page 35.

Perhaps that makes him sound superficial and shallow, Jenny. Perhaps he was superficial, but in the nicest possible way. There were no dark secret places in Laurie. He was frank and straightforward. He was open and honest and not ashamed to share himself with anyone.

How can I describe him to you? How can I make you see him through my eyes?

Perhaps I'd be jumping the gun to try. I wasn't sure exactly how I saw him myself at that stage, those first few weeks.

He was so different, Jenny, so very different from your father, from any man I had known. I suppose it was natural, really, that we had lunch together most days. Even your father thought so, Laurie and I being the only ones in the office then, apart from Cathy, who went off with her friends at midday.

What wasn't so natural, maybe, was the way I came to look forward to those lunch-times, to think each evening about the things we'd said that day, and to wonder what we'd do tomorrow.

Most times we just went to the pub, to have a cider and a toasted sandwich, and to talk. Other times we bought ham rolls and went to the park, and talked.

Occasionally, once in a while, we would do something crazy, like that terribly hot day during the summer when Laurie bounded out to the front office, swinging the washroom towels.

"Let's take an extra hour and go swimming, cool off a bit," he suggested, pulling the sheet I was working on from my typewriter.

I frowned at him. "Don't be silly, Laurie. We can't."

"Anyway," I went on, "we haven't got costumes."

"So we'll buy them," he said, as if I were a child who couldn't see the obvious, and he bundled me out of the office before I could protest further.

The only other people in the pool were a party of schoolchildren, and, do you know, Jenny, I didn't feel one bit older than them as we larked about in the water!

Afterwards we went to a cafe and had hot dogs and a cool drink. There was a jukebox in the corner, and Laurie put money in and we picked three records to play.

I can't remember the first two. But I'll never forget the third one. It was an instrumental called "Petite Fleur" and Laurie whistled it as we sauntered back to the office, slipping my hand into his as we crossed the busy junction at George Street.

I don't know why I should mention that, Jenny. It wasn't so unusual. Laurie would often lean a hand on my shoulder as I pointed out a clause in a contract, or take my arm as we negotiated the city streets. He was just — just friendly.

Perhaps, subconsciously, I realised there was something different about the touch of his fingers that time, and that's why it stuck in my mind.

ALL THAT MIGHT HAVE BEEN

THE next morning when I came in to work there was a little pink rose lying on my desk, and a scribbled message on the top sheet of copy paper. *Une petite fleur pour ma petite fleur.*

I don't think I reacted much at first, Jenny. I just sat there staring at it, wondering whether to feel embarrassment or pleasure. Maybe I felt a bit of both, until Laurie came through, grinning in mock sheepishness, and dispelled the former by saying the park keeper had chased him for 200 yards when he'd pinched it on his way to the office.

We both laughed then, and I was able to cluck disapprovingly.

But it wasn't really funny. That was the first time a man had given me a flower, Jenny. Your father wasn't the sort of person who would ever think of such a thing, and the few boys I knew before I met him would have considered it "cissy".

Ma petite fleur. I told myself it was just nice, silly nonsense, but I took it home and pressed it between the pages of that big anthology of verse that sits on top of the bookcase.

I wondered if Laurie ever read poetry. Your father didn't, certainly.

Maybe it was disloyal of me to compare the two of them, but in those days I couldn't help it. Laurie, with his shaggy, too-long hair, and pink shirts, and bright and breezy manner. Jim, with his short-back-and-sides, his neatly-pressed business suit, tie always exactly in place.

Poor Jim. He would have died of embarrassment at the thought of holding my hand in public. He could no more have pinched a flower from the park than — than Laurie could have kept silent for two consecutive minutes.

It was when summer had gone and we were well into the autumn that Laurie and I went to Hillingford one morning. We were getting specifications for a country house that was going on his books, and afterwards we went to a hotel for lunch.

It was a very elegant, out-of-town place, somewhere he occasionally took clients he was anxious to impress. Oak panelling covered the walls, and there was an aura of solidity, of old-fashioned grandeur, about it.

"I'm not surprised they're impressed," I told him. "It's beautiful, I love it."

"Ah, but you should see it at night, by candlelight," Laurie said. "They clear away the dance floor, and they've got three little old men playing drums, sax and piano."

He reached across the table and touched the little finger on my right hand.

"Come and have dinner with me, Susan."

I moved my hand away, picked up a wine glass and sipped from it.

"Don't be an idiot, Laurie, I've got a husband and daughter, as

you very well know."

"What's that got to do with anything?" he asked easily. "There's nothing in the marriage vows about 'forsaking all other dinner partners', is there?"

He droned the words in a deep, clerical voice, and I smiled for a moment, then shook my head.

"No, Laurie, it's just not on. How on earth would I explain it to Jim?"

In the event, I didn't have to explain anything. I wonder what strange fate decreed Jim would be away on business that Friday night — the same night as your Aunt Audrey wanted you to go over for your cousin Anne's party and stay till Saturday with them.

It was a wonderful evening, Jenny, that Friday. How can I make you see it? It was just — just so right.

The restaurant was marvellous, the food good, and the dancing fun.

Have you ever had an evening like that, Jenny? Surely everyone must, at least once in a lifetime.

"Laurie, it was —" I started to say when he dropped me off at home, but I stopped, unable to find a word that wouldn't trivialise the experience. Words didn't matter anyway. Laurie knew exactly how it had been.

"We'll do it again, shall we?" he said.

"No . . . no, we won't, Laurie. We mustn't. Tonight was different. But next time — or the next again — I would have to lie to Jim about it, and I can't do that."

"Then don't," he said simply. I turned to him in the car, and his eyes had lost that glimmer of humour.

"Don't lie," he went on. "Tell him. Tell him I love you and I want to marry you. Tell him you're leaving him."

Have you ever felt you're in some kind of echo chamber, Jenny? Where the words are bouncing all around you, but you've no idea where they're coming from? Then — "Stop it, Laurie," somebody was saying. "Don't do this, please.

"I've got a daughter, a little girl of five who has my green eyes and Jim's funny sort-of-squashed nose, and — and —"

"Bring her with you." The answer bounced back. "I'll love her, Susan, I promise. I love her already, because she's a part of you. I'll make her happy. I'll make you both happy."

So many words, Jenny. So many words. Eventually, I stopped listening to them because they weren't important any more. All that mattered was Laurie's arms around me, and his eyes seeking mine, making me acknowledge something I had avoided for months.

I almost made up my mind that weekend. You didn't return from Audrey's until lunch-time on Saturday, and your father wasn't due home until the evening. So I had time to think, time to agonise and rationalise and yearn for solutions that weren't possible.

But by Saturday night I had almost made up my mind. Almost . . . until Jim returned, and you ran to meet him, and he threw you high into the air, up and up, almost to the sky, just like my father had done with me.

"Daddy, we had jelly and ice-cream at the party, and sausages on sticks, and little biscuits with funny stuff on them," you told him. "And Mummy let me wear my green dress, the one with the ribbons, and Auntie Audrey said —"

I didn't hear what Auntie said. I just looked at you in your father's arms, and at the silent love and pride in his tired eyes as he listened to your chatter . . . And I knew I couldn't do it, Jenny. I could never take you from him and deprive you of the father you loved.

I LOOK towards the altar. Peter is looking anxious now, glancing at his watch and muttering to Robin, his best man. I try to catch his eyes, smile, reassure him that nothing is wrong. It's traditional for the bride to be late, and you're determined to do the right thing, Jenny.

I tried to do the right thing, too, love, when I saw Laurie at lunch-time on Monday and handed him the shakily-written letter that told him I was leaving.

"But it's for the wrong reasons!" He tore the slip of paper in two and caught me by the shoulders.

"Don't do it, Susan. Not for those reasons. One day, Jenny will grow up. She'll get married and she'll leave you, and then you'll regret it, Susan. You'll regret all that could have been."

I shook my head and backed away from him, and the tears in my eyes must have spilled over just then, for Laurie's expression softened and he reached out a hand to wipe my cheek.

"Don't cry, lovey. Please don't cry, or you'll have me crying, too."

He stared at me for a long time, then he smiled crookedly. It was an 'oh-well-you-win-some-lose-some' smile.

"Go home, Susan, if that's what you're going to do. Don't worry about anything. Just go home — quickly . . .

"And try to be happy."

Be happy? I walked two stages before catching the bus, then sat there in the front seat, staring out of the window.

I set out the milk and biscuits for you coming home from school, and listened to you reading homework from "Janet and John Book Two".

I made dinner and washed up, and then I told your father I was leaving my job at the agency.

He didn't say much about that, then or in the weeks that followed. But perhaps he understood more than I knew, for there was a strange gentleness about him after that.

Sometimes I would glance up to see him looking at me with something like fear in his eyes, and he would turn away quickly, as if guilty of intrusion in something that was none of his business. Yet it was his business — his happiness was at stake, too.

NOT that I was aware of all that then. It was only in retrospect that I thought it might be so. I wasn't aware of anything much then, Jenny, except a feeling that whatever joy life might have held was over, and that only duty remained . . .

. . . Until just after your sixth birthday, that is. That was the year you developed pneumonia, and were so terribly, desperately ill. Suddenly there was no place in my thoughts for Laurie and what might have been. There was only blind terror . . . and guilt.

I still remember the moment when the doctor told us you had passed the crisis and would pull through. I cried then. For the first time in months I sat down in a chair and let the sobs rack my body until there were no tears left within me.

Your father held me tightly, rocking me in his arms, murmuring words that didn't mean anything.

"It'll be all right, Susan," he crooned when I had stopped crying. "You'll see. Everything will be all right now. She'll come home soon, and then we'll do things together, just the three of us.

"I've got a new assistant manager starting soon, so I won't have so much work, and there'll be more time for — for everything.

"You'll see, Susan. I promise. Everything will be all right now."

It wasn't, of course. Not at first. But it started to get better after that, slowly, stage by stage.

He was so patient, Jenny. He tried so hard, learning to do things that were unfamiliar to him, sharing emotions that he found so difficult to put into words. And I was grateful, and strangely moved.

There was a growing closeness at that time, a closeness we had never known, even in the early days of marriage. Perhaps that was because we both knew sorrow and sorrow, even for different reasons, can be a bond.

Yet another bond, that is, for after your illness I realised that we had so many. There was you, of course. And the house that together we had made a home.

And nine years of marriage, common experience, joint hopes. That counts for a lot, Jenny. You'll discover that for yourself when you start to build these things with Peter.

He is looking suddenly tense, and I turn to see a flurry of activity at the church door. The organ is striking up, and now "The Bridal March" is playing and we are all on our feet.

"O Perfect Love". That's the first hymn, and I can see by the way Jim's lips are moving that his throat has dried up, and he is only miming. Yet he looks calm as he stands out there by the altar, waiting to do his bit when the minister asks who giveth this woman.

That theirs may be
The love which knows no ending,
Whom Thou for evermore
Dost join in one.

This is the moment Laurie warned me about, so long ago now, it seems.

Have I felt regret these last years, Jenny?

Sometimes, perhaps. Or, no, regret is the wrong word. Sadness would do better. Yes, sometimes I have felt a sadness for what might have been.

Just sometimes, when I hear a song from time to time, and I remember how the words of every song then seemed to have been written especially for me.

And sometimes when I am alone, and I take that crumbly, discoloured rose from the anthology of verse. *Ma petite fleur.*

Yes, there have been moments of sadness — like the time I bumped into Pat Owen in Chester Street, and she told me Laurie had married two years previously. Had I heard? Did I know he had little twin boys now? Pat laughed, and said even the responsibilities of fatherhood hadn't changed him one whit.

I felt such a stab of pain then, and afterwards, remorse — for I should have been glad that Laurie was happy.

But — regrets, Jenny? No, on the whole I have never regretted it. How could I, when I turn my head and see Daniel sitting at the back, his duties as usher complete? He did very well for his 13 years, officiously directing his big sister's guests, enjoying the importance of his rôle in the proceedings.

I must have missed the minister asking who giveth this woman, for suddenly I hear Jim saying, "I do." Then, his part over, he steps back and joins me in the front pew.

His hand shakes slightly as he lays down the hymn sheet, and I realise how very nervous he must have been.

But he smiles, takes my hand and squeezes it, and I return the pressure of my fingers.

No, Jenny. I definitely have no regrets. □

Complete
Story
by
SARAH
BURKHILL

All That's Left Unsaid

**Like most of us, she thought of the
things she wanted to say, now
when it was too late.**

I'D meant to get Dad's place straightened up
this morning, but I had so long to wait at the
health centre that time has gone by and I've
done nothing.

It had been Greg's idea that I should see the
doctor, although I hadn't wanted to go, but he
insisted so much that it was easier just to agree
and let him make an appointment for me.

"I know you don't like going, Anna, but you
must," he'd said. "Everything's been such a strain
for you this week . . . ."

ALL THAT'S LEFT UNSAID

"Dr Jamieson can give you something to help you cope," he added, "to make it easier."

To make it easier! How can anything a doctor prescribe ever make a bereavement easier? Will three tranquillisers a day stop you missing the father you've loved for 28 years?

"Yes, I know," Greg said, squeezing my hand. "But see the doctor anyway, love. Let him take a look at you."

So I did as he wanted, and that's why it's half past two and I still haven't made a start. I don't really know where to begin, that's the trouble.

Greg has helped — he's already cleared out the cupboards, packed away some domestic equipment and generally tidied up. But there are some things I can't let him do — like sorting through Dad's personal belongings, all his bits and pieces.

It's only three years ago that he moved in here. Keeping on his little flat had seemed silly when Greg and I had the upper floor of the house lying empty, and it could so easily be converted to give him complete privacy.

A sort of granny-house, that's what it would be, I told him. But he didn't like the cissy-sounding name, so Greg jokingly christened it Lindsay's Loft. That's what it's been ever since.

How Dad loved this place — how well he settled in. Looking around me now, I don't really believe he'll never be back again. I can't think I'll never see him sitting in that chair by the fire, reading a book from the shelves he put up in the alcove.

I bought a new book for him when I was in town last Tuesday, but he never saw it.

When I got home I was busy with other things, and by the time I remembered, he'd had that massive coronary.

NOW I don't know what to do with all those books on the shelves — or with the other things. The painting-by-numbers set he bought last winter when he decided to "take up art." His lovingly-carved figures on the mantelpiece — the squirrel with the nut between its paws, the Arab dhow.

And his beautiful old mandolin, lying in the corner. He never did learn to play it properly, but every week he spent ages polishing the fine old wood and ivory inlay until it glowed and almost looked alive.

It seems cruel and unfeeling to move these things — as if he might come in at any moment, and want something, and find it missing.

On the table by the window are two pages of notepaper, a letter he had started to Uncle Jack, and never finished. But then Dad never completed letters, anyway. He would write about a page and a half, then decide he'd tear it up and phone instead.

"The trouble with letters is that everything I want to say seems too trivial to put down on paper," he would complain. "I mean, things like — like having a pint with Harry Dixon after our bowls game, or you making baked apples and bringing one up for me to have after my tea.

"Those are the sort of things that are important to me, but it seems daft writing them down."

I fold the pages in half, but I don't know what to do with them and they're still in my hand as I walk through to the little bedroom.

It's tidy in here. Greg must have put away the clothes that were lying about — Dad always had an assortment of shirts or jackets draped over chairs. I used to tease him about it and he'd wave me away and tell me to stop fussing him.

One of his navy-blue socks is lying on the floor by the bed. Greg must have missed it. I pick it up, and notice there's a hole in the toe. Why didn't he tell me? I could have darned it for him, or got him a new pair.

Instead, he spent his last day wearing a sock with a hole in it.

Suddenly, that seems the saddest thing in the world, and I want to cry, to shed the first tears since that awful day. I still can't, though, so instead I sit down on the bed, hugging that old woollen sock like a child getting comfort from a piece of rag.

But you're not a child, Anna. You're 28 years old. You're grown up.

Maybe that's part of the trouble. Perhaps I could cry if the tears were for Dad alone. But they wouldn't be, I know, they would be partly for myself, too. Because I feel alone and frightened, and because it's the . . . the end of something.

The end of my youth, perhaps.

SOME people believe that you're never truly grown up while you still have a parent living — until then you're still someone's little boy or girl, and can behave accordingly.

Now, suddenly, I am catapulted into adulthood. Now I'm supposed to be really grown up.

But I don't feel it, even now. I feel lost and bewildered, just like I did when I was 13 and my mother died. That time I was able to run to my father, and hide away from everything in his strong, comforting arms.

He took me on his knee then, and we sat like that for hours, the two of us.

It's funny, really. At that age, when things go wrong, it's so lovely to be treated as a child. It's wonderful to have a *proper* grown-up person to shoulder all the responsibility, and tuck you up in bed, and kiss you, and tell you everything will come right eventually.

Yet, at other times, when all is well in your 13-year-old world, you resent being babied, and feel bitter at not being taken seriously.

Oh, how often I felt like that! Does everyone? I wonder. I expect so. Adolescence, they call it — that disease of the teens just as measles and mumps are usually the diseases of childhood.

Some people thought it would be worse for me, having no mother, but I was never aware of it being so. We were very close, Dad and I. But in spite of that — or perhaps because of it — we still had all the usual troubles through that long haul of growing, of change and experimentation.

I thought grown up was something you became when you were 21 — that suddenly, at that magic age, everything became clear.

At 21 you would be transformed overnight into a competent, capable adult, able to take life in your stride, to cope with every problem that presented itself.

Then, when that milestone was past and nothing happened, I decided adulthood must come when you got married and had a home of your own.

But I didn't feel grown up then, either, as Dad led me down the aisle in a flurry of white organza. Or later, even, when Greg and I came home and moved into this big old house his aunt had left him.

There is a noise in the other room, and I jump up, startled. Then I realise it's only the clock, chiming the half-hour. Greg will be home quite soon, and I should be downstairs seeing to the dinner.

But I feel reluctant to leave now, as if here, perhaps, Dad can be with me, reading my thoughts and knowing all the things I long to tell him.

Why do we seldom speak when we have the opportunity? Why do we only think of all the things we want to say, when it's too late to do so?

Perhaps, like Dad's attitude to letter-writing, it's because some things sound daft when they're put into words. Things like "Thank you for being there", for instance. And things like "I love you". When was the last time I told him that? When I was nine, ten — thirteen, maybe? A long time ago, anyway. Before the years made me slightly embarrassed by emotion.

Oh, he knew, I don't doubt it. But that isn't the point. I didn't tell him. And now I'll never be able to tell him anything again . . .

"How did you get on at the doctor?" Greg is saying, as I dish out the meal. "Did he give you something?"

"No," I tell him firmly. "Dr Jamieson doesn't believe in tranquillisers any more than I do. Anyway, he says it's only to be expected, me being a bit depressed and run down."

He's staring at me, and I can see the thoughts going through his mind, the helplessness there. But he doesn't pursue it, and I'm glad about that.

"Bill Duncan's been promoted to head of publicity," he says instead. "You remember Bill Duncan? Big fellow, with ginger hair and glasses. You met him at the dance last year."

I nod. Yes, I remember, but it's not important. Greg is only trying to bring some normality back to our life, discussing everyday, commonplace things like we used to.

"That was a nice chop. The new butcher seems to be quite good." He pushes his plate away and looks expectant. "Are we having a pudding?"

"Yes, it's baked apples."

I get up to take them from the oven, then stare in horror at the baking sheet as I lift it out. "I forgot, Greg. I forgot! I made three. I made one extra, just like I always do. For Dad."

He is beside me in moments, holding me in his arms as the tears finally roll down my cheeks. He murmurs soft, meaningless words in my hair.

"Oh, lovie, lovie. That's it, just cry. You should have cried before, it's been too long. You've got to go through the grief, not shut it all up."

I ease myself from his arms a little, and reach into my pocket for a paper tissue.

"It's not just that. It's not as simple as that. It's — it's a whole lot of things — different, mixed-up things.

"It's a hole in his sock — and a half-written letter — and a book that I forgot to give him on Tuesday — and . . . and all the things I never told him — and now we're going to have a baby, and he doesn't *know*!"

I SENSE the new tension in Greg's arms, and I realise that this isn't the way I should have told him. It should have been such a wonderful moment, this culmination of all our hopes these last years.

I move away slightly, and look up at him. "Are you pleased?"

He is quiet, so many different expressions mingling on his face.

"Yes, of course I'm pleased," he says eventually. "I think it's the most marvellous thing in all the world. It's what we want. What we both want. Isn't it?"

Yes. It's what we want. At any other time I would have been over the moon. And even now, I *am* happy about it.

But it's just that — oh, how can I make him understand this confused jumble of thoughts that I don't even understand myself?

"I just wish he'd known," is all I say.

"I think — I think maybe he did, in a kind of a way," Greg says slowly. He goes off to rummage in the hall cupboard.

ALL THAT'S LEFT UNSAID

"Look at these. I found them in a drawer upstairs, when I was cleaning it out yesterday."

I undo the string on the net carrier he has passed me, and tumble the contents out.

There are perhaps 20 of them — little wooden building blocks, beautifully planed and varnished. Each one is decorated on all sides with a variety of carvings — birds, apples, a lion's head, a boat.

They're perfect. Solid and enduring, not like anything you can get

A CHILD'S SMILE

Painted with the colours
  of dawn,
Reflected in the pearly skies,
Lips the shade of softened
  peach,
Sapphires in her happy eyes.
The mysteries of years all
  gathered there
In the baby smile that
  we share.

Bitter winds will lose their
  bluster,
Ice melt to the scent of
  morning dew,
Forgotten is the icy bite of
  winter
When the baby smiles at
  you.
She knows she has you in her
  loving grip
With one pucker of her
  baby lips.
— A. R., Thornton Dale.

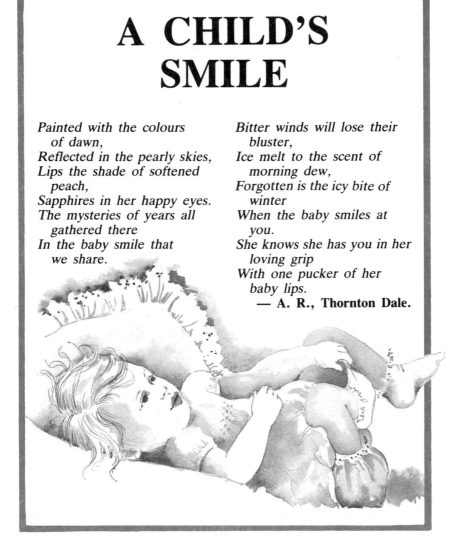

in the shops. I pick up each one slowly, and feel its solidness.

Greg runs a hand through his hair and looks suddenly awkward and embarrassed.

"Anna, I'm not saying he knew about *this* baby. I know he couldn't have. But — well, he must have believed that one day he would have a grandchild. Maybe not this year, or the next. But one day.

"Perhaps he even knew that when that day came he wouldn't be around, and he wanted the baby to have something of his — a part of him. And that's why he made these."

He tails off, flushing slightly, and I pick up another of the little cubes. It's one with an elephant on the side.

Suddenly another picture comes into my head. A picture of a round-cheeked, smiling baby boy or girl, picking up the blocks, laughing, mixing them up, knocking them down delightedly when I have put each on top of the other.

And suddenly, for the first time, I can see this tiny speck of life inside me as an identity. As a proper little person, loved already, not just a terrifying responsibility I feel slightly unequal to.

"A part of him . . . " I repeat. "Oh, Greg, the baby will have so much of him, won't it? It'll have these bricks that he made with love. And it'll have all the memories of him, all that I can give it.

"Oh, and his name, too," I say excitedly. "Greg, I want the baby to have his name!"

He smiles gently. "Even if it's a girl? A girl called Richard?"

I smile back at him. "Don't be silly. No, Lindsay if it's a girl."

We abandon the baked apples along with the dirty dishes and other kitchen clutter, and go through to the sitting-room. Greg pulls me down on to his knee, and I cling to him as if I were a child. Me, Anna Sinclair who is soon to have a child of her own!

Maybe I'll feel grown up when I'm a mother, I think now.

But perhaps I won't. Perhaps no-one ever does, and it's all just a myth invented for the young to give them something to aim at.

It doesn't matter, anyway. Not now. Because now I feel . . . hopeful, contented, capable of looking forward, and of going forward.

And that's more important than feeling grown up, I think. Or perhaps — perhaps it's just the same thing. □

**Complete
Story
by
ISOBEL
STEWART**

When

**Nothing had been said between them — but
by the end of her stay here, a decision would have
been made that could affect their
future together . . .**

Stars Begin To Fall

BECAUSE it was late afternoon everything at the beach cottage looked different. Sarah had never been there at this time of year when no-one else was around. High tides had swept the beach, revealing rocks she had never seen before.

Donald had driven her down to the cottage. It had been a pleasant journey and they had brightened the three-hour drive by discussing Lynn and Peter's wedding. How beautiful their daughter had looked!

And Sarah had reminded Donald of the list of instructions she had given to Jenny, their youngest child. What fun Jenny would have looking after her father and the house.

Before he left to drive back home, Donald had said, "I wouldn't feel so bad about leaving you if Mac were here."

Then he had kissed her and left.

Now, looking out the window, Sarah realised it was the mention of their old dog that was troubling her. She couldn't put him out of her mind.

I'm even more foolish than I thought, she told herself, moving away from the window and the memories of a black spaniel running along the beach, his wet ears flying in the wind. I hardly cried when my daughter was married, and yet I have this terrible ache inside for Old Mac.

Mac had died, peacefully, a month before the wedding, but there was so much to do in those last few weeks she hadn't had time to dwell on it.

Here at Fairhaven she would be aware all the time that he was gone, for he loved it here, spending hours down on the beach with the children.

Right now, Sarah told herself, I'm going for a walk along the beach, because the longer I put it off, the harder it will be. So she wrapped up well and set out into the bracing wind.

WHEN she got back to the cottage, she made an omelette for herself, then put a match to the logs in the fireplace, the wood they had collected during the summer.

That big log there, she thought. Lynn and Peter had found it last summer.

Gazing into the brightness of the flames, Sarah thought about the young couple.

I am so very glad, she thought. I have no fears about the way they feel towards each other. It's a lasting love. And as she remembered the wedding and the breathless wonder on the two young faces, tears came to her eyes.

Now that she was alone, there suddenly came the thought she had been pushing to the back of her mind recently.

When did we last look at each other like that, she thought. Donald and I? How many years, how much living together will it take before the children lose that special feeling?

And the saddest thing of all, she thought, is that you don't even realise it has gone.

The next day the memories of Mac were no less painful as she walked along the beach.

The rest of the day went as she had planned. She slept well that night, waking to thoughts of another peaceful, solitary day spent walking alone on the beach.

It was almost with a feeling of outrage she saw the young man on the beach that morning. He was walking, as she was, with his head down against the wind, hands thrust deep in his pockets. He was young, blond and lean hipped. Sarah felt her heart sink at the thought of even having to pass the time of day with a stranger. But to her surprise, he seemed just as put out to see her as she was to see him, and he only gave her a curt nod as he passed.

That afternoon she was dismayed to hear someone knock at her door. It was quite cold by then, and she had lit the fire.

Reluctantly, she opened the door.

The young man she'd seen earlier on the beach stood at the door, a seagull in his arms, its feathers sticky with oil.

"Have you any detergent?" he asked her. She saw that his face was tight with anger.

"Yes," she said. "Wait a minute." She put some detergent into a plastic basin, filled it with water and carried it outside.

Together they began to wash the seagull. Strangely, it didn't struggle; it almost seemed to know that they were helping it.

They changed the water in the basin twice, and then there was nothing more they could do.

"I think he'll make it now," the man said. "Come on, let's see if he'll fly."

He strode ahead down to the beach, carrying the gull in his arms. Sarah followed.

For a moment, as they stood at the edge of the sea, he looked down at her as if he were really seeing her for the first time. Tentatively, he smiled and Sarah smiled back.

"Good luck," he said and he let the bird go. Sarah's heart sank as the gull fell to the sand, but then, flexing his wings, he took off, becoming confident.

"He's all right!" she said joyfully.

The stranger looked down at her. "More than you could say for you and me," he remarked. He was covered in oil, and Sarah, looking at herself, realised that her clothes were dirty, too.

"Come and have some coffee," she said on impulse.

"I'd like that," he agreed. "Look, I'm staying just over the dunes from you, at the Carsons' cottage. You put the kettle on, and I'll go back and change first."

They walked back up from the beach together and parted where the path forked. Sarah changed into clean jeans and a jersey, then towelled her damp hair dry. She had just set out two mugs of coffee and some biscuits when he arrived.

"A fire," he said with pleasure. "And home-made biscuits."

"Not made here," Sarah admitted. "I brought them from home."

He held out his hand. "We'd better introduce ourselves. I'm Steve Johnson. The Carsons are old friends of my parents."

They sat down close to the fire.

"I'm Sarah Wade," she told him. "I'm sorry if I was a little unfriendly on the beach this morning. I didn't think there would be anyone else here this time of year."

"Neither did I," Steve admitted. "And I certainly wasn't too pleased to know I didn't have it all to myself."

He hesitated. "I've got myself in something of a tangle. Jobwise — and girlwise. I came down here to try to see things more clearly."

"My eldest daughter got married last week," Sarah told him. "After all the excitement, I needed a rest."

He smiled and the momentary stiffness between them left.

"I understand that," he agreed. "That's how I felt, too."

Sarah poured them each another cup of coffee and they chatted.

He was an English teacher, he said, and he had always thought that some day he would like to write a book. Now, suddenly, he was beginning to wonder if that time would ever come.

"I can see myself, years from now," he said slowly, "teaching my classes and still telling myself that one day I will write that book. And I'll wish that I was free to do what I wanted."

"Do you dislike teaching?" Sarah asked him.

"Oh no," he said, surprised. "I enjoy it. Of course there are days when the kids get me down, but there are other days when I get a spark of response from just one of them, and that's enough to keep me going."

Steve told her about his girlfriend, Marianne. She was a teacher too, he said, and their love hadn't been one of these sudden things; it had started as friendship and had grown slowly. Now, though, he had to come to a decision.

It was very simple, he said. Marianne wanted marriage — but he didn't think he was ready for it.

He shrugged. "Maybe after a week here I'll know whether it's her way or mine."

Sarah lifted her head. "It's not a battle you're fighting."

He stared at her, astonished, and then threw back his head and laughed.

"Sarah, you're right," he said. "And maybe that's a starting point." He stood up in one easy movement. "Thanks for the coffee."

The cottage seemed very quiet after he had gone.

IT rained that night, but Sarah read for a while and worked on a sweater she was knitting for Jenny. She slept well again.

The rain had stopped by morning, but it looked as if there might be more later, so she went out along the beach early, making her way to the headland. Steve joined her.

The wind was still strong and talking was impossible. But it was pleasant, she realised, just to have company.

That afternoon, he brought her some fish he had caught, and she said that she would grill the fish if he'd like to stay.

As they sat by the fire that evening, and talked, Sarah told Steve about Mac.

"I suppose you'll think I'm the sentimental one now," she said, "when I tell you that I have this ache inside every time I sit at that

rug in front of the fire . . . because I remember how Mac chewed that constantly when he was a puppy."

"Don't be ashamed of loving your old dog, Sarah," Steve said gently. "And don't be ashamed of grieving for him."

It was the gentleness in his voice that was her undoing as the tears came at last — the tears she had been holding back ever since she'd come to the cottage.

Steve held her while she wept and, when at last she stopped, he dried the traces of the tears from her cheeks with his handkerchief.

"Feel better?" he said gently.

She thought about it. She was exhausted and her head ached from crying, but — "Yes," she said, surprised. "I do feel better."

This time he made the coffee, and, after he had finished his supper and said goodnight, Sarah sat thinking by the embers of the fire.

Slowly she began to see that she had been crying not only for the old dog, but for Lynn and Jenny growing up, and for the way the love between Donald and her had changed.

She had been crying, she thought, for all the years that were gone.

And somehow, having admitted the need to cry for these things, it was easy to accept them and to go on.

Steve told her the next day that he'd decided not to give up teaching. He really liked it, he said, those special moments were worth it.

Sarah asked him if he would care to have supper with her, and as they sat beside the fire, he talked again about Marianne and about his doubts.

It was the binding feeling of marriage that bothered him, he said slowly. He had seen so many marriages lose the magic they once had and become humdrum.

Sarah, remembering her own thoughts when she saw the look on her newly-wed daughter's face, could say nothing for a little while. Then, looking at Steve's bent head and his untidy hair, she knew that she must.

"I think," she said, feeling for the right words, "it comes down quite simply to whether you want to spend the rest of your life with that one person. Either you want to marry Marianne, or you're prepared to lose her and take a chance on finding something better with someone else.

"Do you love her, or don't you? It's as simple as that."

It *is* simple, she realised, thinking of herself and Donald. Our lives have changed, *we* have changed. But — I still love him.

"Yes," Steve said, his voice low. "Yes, I love her. I think I'd better marry her."

Sarah had to laugh. "Yes, I think you'd better. And, Steve, you're right. Marriage does change things, but — it can still be good."

THE next morning Steve knocked at her door early. He had a rucksack with him and he told her that he was going back earlier than he had planned.

"To ask Marianne to marry me," he said.

"I'm glad," Sarah said, meaning it. "I'm so glad, Steve."

He looked down at her. "Thanks for everything."

Sarah watched until he was out of sight and, suddenly restless, she wished that the next two days were over and that Donald would come to take her home.

Her lonely morning walk along the beach only increased her longing to go home. So when she climbed the path from the beach and saw Donald's car outside the cottage, she thought for a moment that she was just imagining it.

But it was real, just as his arms around her were real a moment later, when he opened the door and came to kiss her.

He looked down at her. "I managed to get time off work after all, and — I've got something for you," he said a little awkwardly. "A present."

He took her hand and led her into the cottage. He had lit the fire, and there, on Mac's old rug, was a puppy, busily chewing the corner Mac had once chewed.

The dog was small, white and fluffy — completely unlike Mac.

"I don't know what kind he is," Donald confessed. "I was walking past the pet shop and he sort of looked at me. I just walked in and bought him for you. He's . . . different," he said unnecessarily.

"He certainly is," Sarah said. She knelt down and the puppy came to her. She knew as she felt the small, rough tongue that this dog would make his own place in her heart.

"Are you all right?" Donald asked anxiously.

She nodded. "I'm all right," she said, holding the little dog close to her.

That night, before they went to bed, Sarah put a cardboard box beside the fire for the puppy.

"We'd better take him out," Donald said. They opened the door and walked around the cottage as they had always done with Mac.

"Do you remember," Sarah asked, "all the years when we had to lift sleepy babies and take them to the potty? Now —" She laughed, but her laughter was shaky. "Now it's a puppy."

He put his arms around her. "Yes, love, I remember."

And suddenly it wasn't difficult to say all the things she wanted to say.

"What happened to all those years, Donald?" she asked, looking up at him in the moonlight. "Where did they go? What . . . what happened to us? When did we stop being young . . . eager . . . passionate? When did we change?"

He didn't reply immediately and she waited.

"Yes, we have changed," he said at last. "But . . . I doubt we could have gone on living at such intensity. You think those years have gone and the people we were have gone, don't you?"

He paused, smiling at her. "Well, they haven't really. The people we were have grown into the people we are. It's not lost, love, the passionate eagerness, that youth. But it was just the beginning of it all.

"I still love you, Sarah, and I think you still love me. Differently, yes, but . . . in many ways even more deeply."

Donald took both her hands in his and bent to kiss her, gently at first, and then not so gently. Of course, he's right, Sarah thought with love. Yesterday has made today what it is, and today will become part of tomorrow — all our tomorrows, she told herself, for the rest of our lives. □

Complete Story by ELIZABETH MILNE

IN THE QUIET OF THE NIGHT

**They found comfort in their friendship —
a child with no family to care
for her, and a young woman whose
family cared too much.**

H OW old is she anyway?" Tom asked.
I stopped waving when the boat turned side-on as it
left the quay, taking Auntie Ellen, still leaning on
the rail, out of our sight.

"That's a funny question," I said.

"Is it?" Tom turned to walk beside me back to the car,
pulling up the back of my coat collar against the chill wind
off the Irish Sea. "Keep yourself warm now. You've been
standing too long in the cold."

61

IN THE QUIET OF THE NIGHT

"I haven't. I'm fine." I shrugged away his hand. Why should it make me impatient, I wondered. He was only being kind because he was fond of me.

"Why do you want to know?" I asked.

"Know what?" he said.

"Auntie Ellen's age."

"Curiosity. You're pretty close to her, aren't you, in spite of there being such a difference between you?"

"Age-wise, you mean? She's only a bit over forty."

"Oh, come on, love, think again." Tom laughed. "She looks more like sixty."

I paused by the car, frowning, then I got in, reaching for the seat belt. "I'm right. When I was about seven, Auntie Ellen was twenty-one."

Suddenly I saw her again as vividly as she had appeared to my young eyes all those 20 years ago: tall, straight, agile and handsome, the light blue eyes in her tanned, outdoor face smiling down at me, one crooked tooth showing slightly at the corner of her mouth and the thick hair ruffled untidily.

"Well, I suppose she does have to work hard on the farm," Tom was saying, "but surely they have help, and life must go slowly in a place like Balmakeely. There's no rat race, just watching the fish jumping in the river and listening to the donkeys braying in the night."

He laughed.

"Oh, be quiet," I said softly, and was aware he had turned to look at me in surprise.

But I wasn't interested in what Tom might be thinking. In my mind I was back those 20 years, watching and listening to Auntie Ellen.

She wasn't really my aunt. I don't think there was any kinship at all between her family and mine. If there had been, it was certainly too vague a relationship to be explained to the seven-year-old I was then.

I only knew that there was a bond of friendship between my grandmother and Mrs Maloney, Ellen's mother, and that I had been sent from the tenement in Glasgow, where I lived with my grand-parents, to the Maloney farm in the West of Ireland. I was to be pampered and petted and made strong again after a long, dangerous illness.

Mrs Maloney, who told me to call her Mallie, was a heavily-built, heavy-footed woman with a broad, kindly face and greying hair, drawn straight into a big bun on the back of her head. The sleeves of her dark dress were invariably folded up to show sturdy forearms and the dress itself was covered back and front with a sleeveless overall tied at the sides.

Mr Maloney, like his two sons, was a silent, stocky man of formidable strength, seldom without a blackened pipe between his teeth, and a tweed cap pulled over his thick hair. If he ever noticed me, he gave little sign of it.

All of them, Mallie and Ellen, too, wore men's working boots, lacing above the ankles and usually clogged with wet or drying mud, which they scraped off at the back kitchen door before coming into the farmhouse.

I ADORED Ellen from the first day. She was waiting when the guard handed me down from the van at the little country junction. At first I didn't understand what she said, recognising only that the sound of the voice was rich and musical and welcoming.

She took my small bag in one hand and offered me the other. Then, obviously realising that tears were close at hand at the strangeness and weariness of all that was happening around me, she knelt down, put her arms round me and pressed my face into the warmth of her neck.

No kissing — how had Ellen guessed that I'd shrunk from adult kisses ever since my mother had disappeared? All I sought now was a feeling of safety, comfort and friendliness.

"What a white, wee thing to be coming all that long travel on your own! Never mind, there's the trap and there's Micky waiting, and we'll be home in two steps," Ellen said. "Come on now, girl dear."

Micky was a beautiful, light-brown donkey and the trap was a neat two-wheeled cart with a worn, leather cushion along its single seat.

During all the weeks of that visit, Ellen called me nothing other than "girl dear" and I used to try to imitate the tender curl of the words as they came from her tongue.

Like a shortened shadow, equipped with small, heavy boots dug out from the back of some cupboard, I followed Ellen — Auntie Ellen by this time — around the yard and the fields of the farm while she went through her everyday chores.

They seemed never ending — hens' mash to be scraped out, potatoes dug, the cows called in and the calves fed. There was a field of turnips to be singled, the goat to be caught, tethered and milked.

There were pig pails to be filled, then Ellen and I would carry them down to the far muddy corners where the grumphies rooted about.

In spite of the smell, this was the job I liked most, because over the wall of this bottom field there was a thick, high bank of gorse, and beyond it a river.

It was completely hidden, and after a quick look back towards the house to make sure no-one was watching, Ellen would scramble over the wall, haul me after her and, giggling, we would pick our

IN THE QUIET OF THE NIGHT

way along a tiny track through the prickles to the water.

Boots would be tugged off, socks stuffed inside them, and we would find two good flat stones to sit on while we dabbled our feet in the cool, brown stream.

Then Ellen would talk. It was only much later that I realised how little she talked in the house.

But down on the stones by the river, her words ran as quickly as the chattering water. She asked questions about the city, the streets and shops and houses, even about my school.

I couldn't tell Ellen much because, after all, I was just  going on eight and still in the baby classes at school, but I did know which teacher I liked best and how she dressed and did her hair and how she read us stories about places like China, India and Fiji on Friday afternoons.

I could even remember some of the tales and tried to repeat them in my own words to my fascinated listener. Once, she remarked wistfully, "That Miss Henry, hasn't God been good to her! She must be a lovely woman!"

"Miss Henry? The teacher? Oh no, she's not half as lovely as you, Auntie Ellen!"

"There's cobwebs in your eyes, girl dear!" She gave a short laugh. "But it's not just the pretty hair, or the clothes, or the dainty ways I'm thinking about, it's the mind."

I didn't understand, not even when she added, as if talking to herself, "It's her lovely, clever mind that has me burned up with jealousy."

And for a while there the lightness went out of Ellen Maloney's eyes.

IT was Auntie Ellen who finally brought me round to admitting that my mother was dead and not simply gone away on some journey.

"Believing your mam's dead is no bad thing, girl dear," she said quietly. "It's a sad sorrow for you, but that's all a part of life, d'ye see?

"There's sad things and terrible hard things, but great, wonderful things, too, that's all got to be lived with, one way or the other, girl dear. Some of them can be changed if you fight them down, but there's not a mite you can do about dying.

"We all come to it, goodness gracious, girl dear, but we can have a tremendous fine time of life while we still have it."

And she tossed back her bang of hair, laughing up at the sun, and kicked a foot in the water to send a spray of silver drops over me.

I loved her with a deep, unquestioning devotion which only became the stronger when a hint of impatience within the family began to show itself.

I suppose I was quiet by nature, and occasionally they either forgot or didn't notice I was sitting there; or possibly, if they thought about it at all, they assumed that I was too young to recognise an atmosphere.

At these times, Auntie Ellen's face became bony, her lips tucked between her teeth and her jaw set hard. Sometimes, after I was in bed, when a rumble of voices down in the kitchen meant that a neighbour had dropped by to visit, Auntie Ellen would come up to the room which we shared and sit silently by the window in the quiet of the night, and I would be aware of her unease.

ONCE I whispered, "Are you angry, Auntie Ellen?" and she jumped as if she had forgotten I was there.

"Girl dear, you should be sleeping! What's upsetting you?"

"Nothing. It's you."

"Me?" She came over quietly on stockinged feet and sat by the bed. "Ah, sure, I'm a disturbance to the whole world. I'm sorry. Go to sleep now."

"You're not angry, are you?"

"Never with you, girl dear."

She gave a little snort I knew meant scorn. "But wouldn't the Lady herself be tearing Heaven to pieces if she had to put up with what's going on down there?"

"What's going on?"

"Ah, plotting and meddling and making plans as if there could be no other option in the world but what suits them. But it won't suit me!"

Auntie Ellen went to stand by the window. "They'll find out — it won't suit me."

The subdued fierceness silenced me, and I huddled under the quilt.

After a while although it was still early and voices still rumbled below, Auntie Ellen pulled her nightgown over her head, dropped her clothes from beneath it and came to bed, putting her arms around me.

The next day was all wrong. As usual, Auntie Ellen was up and away long before I awoke, but when I went down to the kitchen, she and her mother were facing each other across the wooden table.

IN THE QUIET OF THE NIGHT

"I'll not go! I've told you!" Auntie Ellen exclaimed. "How many times must I say?"

"What harm can it do?" was the reply.

"D'you think I don't know? There's no harm, but it's the end of me!" She was shouting now.

"You're wild, Ellen," Mrs Maloney said. "That kind of talk has no sense to it!"

"I'll not go!"

"Dad says you will."

"Never a doubt of that, but he can't drag me at the end of a rope like some bulling cow!"

Then they noticed me standing there and became quiet. Auntie Ellen stomped to the door, swinging her foot at a wandering hen as she went.

She was unapproachable and I was miserable. Her anger lent her a desperate, blind energy and she tore through her chores, clashing buckets, swilling out the cow barn, hitting out with the rope at a prancing goat.

Except when they intended going to a "hooley" or some other special "do" at night, the two brothers never troubled to change from their working shirts and trousers for the evening meal. But Auntie Ellen always took hot water up to the bedroom and came down in a clean blouse and a different skirt. Her brown cheeks would look polished and her hair would be curling damp over her forehead.

But this particular night, she only scrubbed her hands at the cold-water sink and sat down silently at the table, smelling of the coarse, kitchen soap.

Darren, the older brother beside her, gave her a look but said nothing.

Mallie, leaning over with the potato bowl, sniffed and pursed her lips. "You been down at the pigs?"

"I have."

"You'll have to hurry yourself."

There was a short, tense silence. Her father raised his head from his plate and glanced at the two women in turn. "She knows we're going down the road after?"

Mallie nodded.

"Right then. We'll have ye smelling a bit sweeter than ye are this minute."

Auntie Ellen stared at him, but Mallie spoke first. "She'll be putting on her good blue, Dad . . ."

Auntie Ellen interrupted, looking to her father. "I'm not going down the road."

"The Boyles are expecting us."

"You and Mam can go."

"It's not meself nor your mam that's important. Why d'ye think we're taking you?"

"I think nothing. I'm not going."

There was another pause while everyone at the table looked at her. She shook salt on her potatoes and began to eat.

"And why not?" her father asked gently.

"Because I know too well what's in your mind — Michael Boyle! And I'm having none of it!"

He shook his head.

"I thought I had a daughter with some good sense in her mind, but it looks like I was wrong."

"Dad . . ." She swallowed hard and for the first time her voice shook. "Dad, sure you know this has nothing to do with sense. It's feeling! I don't feel for Michael Boyle . . ."

"And what's wrong with the man?" His voice was still gentle, but now everyone knew this was deceptive.

"What's right with him?" she demanded fiercely. "He's twice the age of me, but I'm to be taken down the road for him and his old mother to look me over as if I was some cattle beast.

"I'm supposed to be strong enough to give him the sons he needs for that fine farm of his, and still be able to slave after his mother because she's getting slow and wants a pair of hands and a young back to take the yard-work and the turf-carrying and the egg-washing off her!

"Is that not a wonderful future for a girl? Should I be down on my knees, being thankful that Michael Boyle is willing to look at me?"

FOR some reason, the torrent of words made the younger brother laugh. "Would ye listen to it? Anybody would think she had the five counties to choose from!"

"Quiet, you!" their father interrupted. "There's one true thing you've said, me girl, and that's about the fine farm and the future there is in it for you.

"Remember, it's all Michael's own, with him being the only son, and you'd be the mistress of the house. The old woman's up in years . . ."

"And with me running at her tail all day, she'll pass the hundred easy!"

Mallie interrupted. "Ah, now, she's not such a bad old soul, you know . . ."

"If she was one of the saints of Heaven it would make no difference!"

"Well, think on this now!" The father's tone had hardened. "What will you be in twenty or thirty years? Mistress of your own good house and a farm that's putting money in the bank, or a sour old maid left behind with the worn-out old trash in this house when your mam and I are gone?

"You know well that Darren and Nora Gill will be making a match of it," her father went on, "and your brother Sean here will be off to your Uncle Frank in New Jersey . . ."

"That won't be tomorrow . . . it'll be years yet!"

Darren turned to her and grinned. "Don't you be counting on that."

"And don't you count on me taking orders in me own home from Nora Gill, with her pink hair curlers and her nylon overalls!" Auntie Ellen snapped.

Darren's knife slammed on the table. "Keep that snake's tongue of yours off Nora!"

"Quiet, the pair of you! You're frightening the child!"

As the voices rose, food stuck in my throat, and now Mallie noticed the tears that were trickling down my face. I was lifted on to Auntie Ellen's knee and felt safer with her hands patting me and my arms tight round her neck.

She stood up with me in her arms still. "Dad, here's a plan. Let me go back across the water with the child when she goes.

"I don't want to be caged here always. I want to try something different, to see bigger places, to — to live wider! I want to learn something! Dad, don't you understand all that I'm talking about?" Auntie Ellen ended.

"St Patrick himself wouldn't understand," the father said. "It's an amazement any one of us here can make head or hoof of what ye want."

AUNTIE ELLEN didn't go along the road that night, nor any of the other nights while I was there, but neither did she come home with me when I eventually went back to Glasgow.

I missed her sorely for a few weeks and wrote copy-book letters to her, but her replies were short and disappointingly written on cheap paper with ragged edges at the top. But soon the life of the city and school had me caught and the memories of hens in the kitchen, the scratching of gorse and the bubble of a river became blurred like an old dream.

Once, a long time later, a snapshot came in a letter to my grandmother. It showed a ramrod Auntie Ellen, standing a head taller than a chunky, grey-haired man who had a white flower in his coat.

"Who's that?" I asked.

"A Michael Boyle. They are married," my grandmother answered and turned a sheet of the letter. "It seems he has a farm next to their own. She has done well for herself."

I looked again at the picture, at Auntie Ellen's stiff figure and dark, bony face with its set lips, and I wondered.

Now, 20 years later, I was sure I knew.

Auntie Ellen, dusty haired and leather skinned, had at last come across the water, if only for a short visit, because her husband had died.

The oldest of her four sons was barely 17 so she couldn't leave the farm for longer than a week. There was only an echo of the old wistfulness in her voice as she explained.

"But isn't there someone to help? Surely you don't still do all that work yourself!"

Auntie Ellen shrugged. "What else? Hasn't it been my life? That, and nursing babbies, and then there was the old woman, and then himself . . ."

"Michael Boyle," I said, and suddenly the memory was vivid of her bitter defiance all those years ago. "You once said, 'What's right with him?' What changed your mind, Auntie Ellen? Why him?"

For an instant, she seemed surprised. "I said that?"

"Yes. I remember so well. There was a terrific argument — the time I stayed with you."

"Big ears, had ye? And you no more than a tadpole in them days."

"But Michael Boyle?" I persisted.

She shrugged again. "He was always fair to me. Come Darren and Nora Gill's wedding and the older folk always on at me — who else was there? The men weren't exactly dropping off the trees in Balmakeely."

Questions were tripping up my tongue, but something in her calm look silenced me.

"Girl dear, we've both added on years since then, haven't ye noticed? Now, who's this fella that's after ye?"

"Tom?" Suddenly there didn't seem anything to say about Tom. He was there, that was all — kind, certainly in love with me, a little dull, if I was honest with myself.

I tried to turn her own words into a kind of joke. "He's always fair to me."

After a moment she nodded, knowing I was being evasive. "To be sure, life itself isn't fair most of the time, so maybe it's good fortune to be able to say that much of a man."

Then Auntie Ellen looked at me and I saw how sadly her blue eyes had faded, how the polished, brown skin had withered and the thick hair had dulled.

"Girl dear," she said, "you're young and clever. You've a good mind that's been fed well with plenty of books and teaching, and I know you've a bit of money of your own.

IN THE QUIET OF THE NIGHT

"There's a whole world of living all about you to choose from," she said slowly, "and no-one at your back pushing you to make up your mind."

She hesitated, then went on. "Can you guess at all what I'm talking about?"

"I think so," I said.

"Then think well. If I don't misjudge it, ye want more in your life than a man to be fair to you. Take the word from an old, ignorant woman and think well, girl dear.

"It's not that I'm against marriage," Auntie Ellen said slowly, "not me, but take your time."

She was so right! She had had no options, but I had!

A finger flicked my cheek.

"Speak up," Tom's voice said. "I'm here."

"Sorry!"

"You were muttering away, dreaming. What's it about?"

"I was . . . remembering things about Auntie Ellen."

He grinned. "She's what I'd call a character. Your genuine soda-bread peasant."

"You think so? She certainly calls herself an old, ignorant woman, but I don't know. Years ago, Auntie Ellen wanted to be . . . oh, I don't know . . . perhaps something like a librarian or a teacher."

"What stopped her?"

"It's too long a story," I said. "She simply didn't have a chance to try."

"Well, no need to go broody over it. She seems content enough now, in an earthy kind of way. Does a fairly prosperous line in potatoes and pigs, doesn't she?

"I'd guess she's a pretty shrewd operator in her own particular field, your Auntie Ellen."

I considered that and decided I agreed. And in some other fields, too, I added mentally.

I'd had some surprisingly good advice today from my shrewd, earthy Auntie Ellen!

"What's funny?" said Tom.

"I was just thinking."

"And smiling. Share the joke."

"Some day, perhaps," I said. "When I've had time to think well about it."

He raised his brows, and shook his head. He would never understand me! And I could see him making up his mind to be indulgent and kind.

I liked him, indeed I did, but . . . *You want more in your life — think well, girl dear!*

I sat back in my seat and looked ahead to the long, straight road rushing towards us and made a silent promise to the young woman so quickly grown old. □

The Spirit Of Adventure

**It rustled through the house like a
spring breeze, re-awakening the soul of one
not-so-young couple to the joy of living.**

THE umbrella glowed like a scarlet begonia in the
rain of a cold afternoon, and she twirled it as
slowly and tantalisingly as one of those Southern belles in a Hollywood musical.

It was young Jameson who saw her first, from the
office window. He emitted a long, slow whistle.

Complete Story by LOUISE BRINDLEY

"Hey, Scott," he said. "Just take a look at that, will you!"

I glanced up from the papers on my desk, and saw a many-petalled frilled umbrella, slowly twirling its way down the rain-swept main street.

The woman carrying it appeared to be the only pedestrian actually walking upright, unconcerned with the weather. Everyone else hurried, scurried, scuttled and butted their way in and out of the shops; there were women with bulging plastic bags which bumped their leather-booted calves, and men in grey macs and dripping headgear.

They all looked tired of life, as though the rain had dampened their spirits.

"Some dish, eh?" Jameson said enthusiastically.

But of course Jameson could afford to show enthusiasm. He was warm and dry for one thing, he'd just been promoted at work for another.

Jameson was unmarried. He was bursting at the seams with youthful zest and ambition, and his trim moustache and beard contained more hair than my entire head now seemed capable of producing.

"Humph!" was all I managed in response, unwilling as a senior member of staff to admit that the scarlet umbrella had struck a chord in my own sober head.

Not that I was concerned, the way young Jameson was, with the glory of conquest, another leggy blonde or brunette to add to his list of telephone numbers.

It was memories that struck chords with me nowadays. Often the strangest things — lamplight on wet pavements, the drone of an aircraft overhead, late-night films on television, the opening tune of "Desert Island Discs".

I had reached the age when every policeman looked young — young enough to be the son my wife, Janet, had died giving birth to.

"Oh, come on, Scottie!" Jameson was fond of teasing me. "You're not that old! At least admit that she's got a smashing pair of legs!"

"Hmmm. But what about her face?"

"That's just it, I didn't see her face." Jameson grinned ruefully. "But those legs, that kind of poise, and the way she handles that umbrella can mean only one thing. She's beautiful, and she knows it!"

"Perhaps she's in love," I said. "Being in love has a way of making a woman appear beautiful."

I remembered that Janet had never walked more proudly, or looked more serenely lovely and complacent than when she was carrying our child.

"I'll never rest until I find out who she is." Jameson craned his neck and pressed his nose to the glass, but the girl with the scarlet umbrella had walked down the street out of our sight.

"Doing anything special tonight, Scott?" Jameson asked at five o'clock when we shrugged into our coats.

"There's a good film on television," I said, feeling my age all of a sudden. "I'll watch it in my room after supper."

"Can't be much fun for you in those digs of yours." He frowned suddenly. "Look, why don't you come out with me tonight? We could have a meal and then go on to a pub and have a few drinks."

"Not tonight, thanks all the same." The last thing in the world I wanted was to bore young Jameson. "It's good of you to suggest it, though, and I'm grateful . . ."

How could I explain to him that I was used to my digs? Roast beef Sundays, rissole Mondays, sausage Tuesdays, fish Wednesdays, lamb chops Thursdays, meat Fridays and then liver and bacon on Saturdays.

I was used, too, to Miss Elizabeth French, my landlady, with her penchant for fawn lambswool sweaters, tweed skirts and sensible shoes. Though I noticed that recently she had taken to wearing perfume — a surprisingly nice scent, too.

Jameson shrugged. "OK, Scottie. See you on Monday?"

I liked Jameson, but what use recounting stories of the past to a young man in love with the here and now? A man on the look-out for smashing legs, and a scarlet umbrella? What would he care about my past — my beautiful dead Janet and dead child?

MISS Elizabeth French, my landlady, was coming downstairs when I walked into her hallway.

"It's raining cats and dogs out," I said mildly.

"Yes, I know it is. I went into town this afternoon." She flushed slightly. "I changed my books at the library, and visited the art gallery."

Why is it, I wondered, that I have never come to terms with Miss French? I liked her, but her painful shyness seemed like a barrier between us, and yet somehow I sensed that Miss French liked me, too.

Her fair skin was almost paper thin, and yet her bone structure was beautiful, and her eyes were a rich, glowing hazel.

Often we began a conversation only to have it ended by Miss French hurrying off in embarrassment, it seemed to me, mumbling an excuse of some sort.

Aware of her impatience today, I asked, "Am I late?"

"Just a little, Mr Scott."

"I'm sorry. The bus was late." I'd given up my car two years ago.

"Supper's almost ready." She edged past me. "So please do hurry."

"Meat pie?" This was Friday.

"No." She flushed scarlet. "It's paella, as a matter of fact."

"Paella? But we've never had paella before!"

"If you don't care for paella, Mr Scott, you've only to say so and I'll make you an omelette." She stared at me defiantly, yet her eyes betrayed her uncertainty.

"Not at all, Miss French," I lied. "I really do like paella very much."

"I suppose you think of me as a stick-in-the-mud, Mr Scott? Really, I despair at times!" She disappeared into the kitchen and I noticed, in astonishment, that she'd changed the usual lambswool sweater for a delicate, embroidered blouse.

What brought all that on, I wondered, as I went upstairs to wash my hands. She seemed so angry, and I had never seen Miss French angry before.

I was still wondering as I sat down to face my fellow boarders at the long dining table. Miss French sailed in, put down the meal, and sailed out again to the kitchen with a defiant toss of her head.

"What's this?" Miss Henrietta Midgley, a retired schoolmistress, probed the plumped-up rice and red peppers with a hostile fork. "Where's the meat pie? I prefer meat pie! Has Miss French taken leave of her senses serving up this — foreign rubbish?"

The gentleman on her left, a retired cleric who read Agatha Christie novels between courses, agreed with her.

"One does expect a certain standard of English cooking in a modest establishment of this kind," he pontificated.

"Come now," I said brightly. "Where's your spirit of adventure? Miss French has obviously gone to a great deal of trouble to tickle our taste buds."

"I don't care to have my taste buds tickled," Miss Midgley announced haughtily.

"Nor I." The Reverend Mr Soames laid down his cutlery defiantly.

"Well, I happen to think that this paella is a splendid change from meat pie." My teeth bit into detested rice and red peppers the way they had once bitten into Janet's mistaken notion of Indian curry, when she'd boiled the rice to the consistency of pudding, and spiced the whole mess liberally with curry paste. I hadn't been able to tell her how much I liked it until I'd drunk three glasses of ice-cold water.

"You are at liberty to think what you like, Mr Scott," said the redoubtable retired schoolmistress. "But I intend to complain. Ring the bell, if you please, Mr Soames."

Mr Soames sighed, put down his Agatha Christie novel and complied. Miss French returned, listened to their complaints, and flounced back to the kitchen, while I continued to plough through the saffron and garlic, peas and prawns with pretended gusto — remembering Janet.

Strange, I thought, if Janet had lived, she might have looked the way Miss French did now. Janet had had high cheekbones, too, and sparkling hazel eyes. But she had not lived long enough to grow slightly wrinkled and harassed with the passing years, nor had her golden hair had time to become laced with grey strands.

But what if Janet, and our son, had lived? I should not be sitting at this polished table in a suburban villa, with an upstairs bed-sitting room full of photographs, a colour television, a shelf full of my favourite books, and little else besides.

I refused the sweet, and went upstairs to my room, a tall, slightly stooping civil servant, with little to look forward to.

I took off my jacket and pushed my arms resolutely into my old plaid dressing-gown, envying the bright young sparks like Paul Jameson; nice kids with their lives before them, ready and eager to step into the shoes of middle-aged men like me.

THE late-night film was Judy Garland's "A Star Is Born". I can't watch it, I thought, remembering Janet crying into my white handkerchief in the back row of the one-and-nines, and her lovely brown eyes brimming with tears as she said, "Oh, Scottie, I love you so much! I'll always love you!"

She was so valiant, my Janet, despite her tears.

I remembered the way she looked up at me with those hazel eyes of hers just before she died.

"There will be another girl some day," she whispered, "capable of loving you just as much as I do. Don't close your heart to love, my Scottie. I wouldn't want you to do that."

But I had closed my heart to love a long time ago. Now, as I sat in my chair in front of the television screen, I wondered if Janet, coming back to earth right this minute, would even recognise me as the flaxen-haired, handsome young man she'd fallen in love with so many years ago.

I might have known, when it came to the crunch, that I would have to switch on my TV set, listen to the opening music of "A Star Is Born" and watch the film.

Later, somewhere beyond the film, I became aware of real grief superimposed upon make-believe. I got to my feet, walked out on the landing, and listened.

That's Miss French crying, I thought.

So much for the bold, dashing Scottie of the past. Now I hesitated, not knowing what to do, as Miss French's tears tore at my heart. This was quite ridiculous! Suddenly I strode forward and knocked at Miss French's door.

"Go away," a voice said.

I opened the door and walked into the room. I might have known it. She was watching "A Star Is Born" too.

"Oh, go away!" She dabbed her eyes with a tissue. "Get out! Get out now, this minute."

"I don't quite understand," I said rigidly. "I heard you crying. I thought . . ."

"I know what you thought, Mr Scott. You thought, poor Miss French!" She rose unsteadily to her feet, and I could not help thinking, in passing, what a remarkably fine pair of legs she possessed.

"Well, I am not poor Miss French any longer! I am sick and tired of you, and Miss Midgley and the Reverend Mr Soames, and I intend giving the lot of you notice to quit my house as soon as possible."

"But why? What have we done?" I stood there helplessly, staring at Miss French against the background of the film and Judy Garland singing her heart out.

"You haven't done anything," Miss French continued. "That's just the trouble. Nobody does anything any more. We're all decaying, Mr Scott! This house is decaying! I am decaying! But I intend to put an end to all that . . ."

"You surely don't mean? You're not going to . . .?"

Miss French actually laughed — the first time I'd heard her, I realised. "Heavens, no! I'm going to start to live for a change! Do you realise, Mr Scott, that I have lived in this smouldering place for the last fifteen years, ever since my parents died?"

"Why, no, Miss French. You have never confided in me before." I wished that I was not wearing my plaid dressing-gown and slippers, and I still had no idea why my landlady was so angry all of a sudden. Though, come to think of it, anger suited her. Such a lovely flush on her cheeks . . .

"Would it surprise you very much, Mr Scott, if I told you how much I have hated meat-pie Fridays? Really, the dreariness of all those meat-pie Fridays! Then, the first time I attempted to break the routine, what happened? Complaints! Nothing but complaints from everyone!"

"I wasn't aware that I had complained, Miss French," I protested.

"You didn't have to! I could see by your face how much you hated my paella. In any case, Mr Scott, you wouldn't have had the guts to complain! If you knew how tired I am of you drooping about this house! I thought you would like me to try something new — after all, you're not retired like the other two. I thought you would understand . . . Now, would you mind getting out of my room? I'd rather like to watch this film in peace."

Her eyes were brimming with tears as she turned away.

"It's a fine thing, isn't it," she sniffed, "when all there is left to do is watch old films on television? When all one can do is remember what life used to be like when one was young and in love?"

So Miss French had lost someone close to her, too, the way I'd lost Janet. I closed the door quietly behind me, and went back to my room.

SHAKEN to the core by my encounter with the irate Miss French, I stared at my face in the mirror. Miss French's words echoed in my mind. She was tired of me drooping about the house. Was that how I really appeared to her?

I saw my reflected image in the glass above the washbasin. The years hadn't changed me all that much, I thought indignantly. And "drooping"! Well, maybe years of bending over a desk in a stuffy office had bowed my shoulders a little. But I most certainly did not droop! Then I remembered Jameson's words that very afternoon. "Oh, come on, Scottie. You're not all that old!"

Women! Who could begin to understand them?

Then, remembering Janet, I thought back to the very few rows we'd ever had. Flare-ups which had somehow, miraculously, brought us to a closer understanding of each other. How, when she'd felt neglected, she would suddenly burst into tears and tell me she hated me — which was really just a different way of saying she loved me. I knew that. Then I would hold her in my arms until she'd calmed down.

Remembering Janet . . . the way she'd sobbed over that spoilt curry, not believing for one moment that I really liked it.

"I could tell by your face that you didn't like it," she'd wailed. "Why couldn't you have said so to me instead of just — just pretending?"

"I suppose you'd have preferred me to come the heavy-handed husband?" I'd snapped through burning lips. "Hurled it across the room, or tipped it upside-down on the table? Is that what you wanted me to do?"

"Yes," she'd yelled at me. "That, at least, would have been a positive reaction! I'd have known I'd made a mess of it!"

"And if I'd done that, you'd have gone up in smoke!" I'd retorted, flinging down my serviette.

It was then it occurred to me that Janet had "gone up in smoke" anyway.

"The trouble with you," she'd accused me, "is that you never really see me at times. You treat me like a child, and I'm not a child, I'm a woman! A fully-grown, intelligent woman!"

She'd rushed out of the room and locked herself in the bedroom.

"Go away." She'd sobbed when I'd tried to make my peace with her. "Go away, Scottie. I hate you!"

THE SPIRIT OF ADVENTURE

"For a grown-up, intelligent woman," I'd shouted through the locked door, "you're behaving remarkably like a spoilt child."

But suddenly, I wasn't remembering Janet any more, I was remembering Miss Elizabeth French, and her over-spiced paella. And yet, in a curious way, Miss French and Janet had merged into one person. Remembering Janet had brought me to a closer understanding of Elizabeth.

Elizabeth. The name felt safe and comfortable on my lips. How long had I been in love with her without knowing it? It wasn't just my digs I was used to, and roast beef Sundays, it was the quiet, hitherto predictable Miss French with her penchant for fawn lambswool sweaters, her bright hazel eyes and that delicate lingering perfume.

I remembered now her beautiful blushing face and the eyes that never quite met mine. Maybe it wasn't embarrassment that made her look away. Perhaps it was in case I saw what was written in them.

I had obviously irritated Miss French, therefore she must care about my opinion. Could it be that she cared about me? Dare I hope that Miss French felt for me what I realised now I felt for her?

I'd better find out right now, before it was too late.

The only trouble was, I decided, as I changed into slacks and a light cashmere sweater, that I had closed my heart to love when Janet died.

I had slipped into anonymity as easily as I slipped into my old plaid dressing-gown, because that was the easiest thing to do when there seemed nothing left to live for, the way that Miss Elizabeth French had slipped into taking in boarders for a living — until a mis-timed paella had caused her to rebel against her circumstances.

THE film was very nearly over as I walked firmly across the landing and knocked at Miss French's door.

"Who is it?" she called.

I didn't reply, simply walked in, drawing back my shoulders as I did so.

She stared up at me, speechless with surprise.

I strode forward, took her hands in mine, and pulled her up from her cretonne-covered armchair, into my arms.

"I don't like paella, Miss French," I said. "Not one little bit. But I do happen to love you very much." And then I kissed her.

"Oh, Mr Scott! Scottie!" she murmured. "Oh, Scottie!"

And suddenly the years fell away. My heart was singing with joy, the way it did when I first held Janet in my arms, and I knew that my lovely Janet was right when she had whispered, "There will be another girl some day, capable of loving you just as much as I do."

But I was old enough and wise enough now not to confuse the past with the present. Not to pretend to love Elizabeth the way I had loved Janet.

This was a new love born of age and experience. A kind of bonus to living, and Elizabeth's slightly greying hair was just as dear to me as Janet's golden hair had once been, in those lovely, careless springtime days of our youth . . .

It was still raining on Monday morning. A light spring shower. I whistled as I shaved, then hurried down to breakfast, and actually grinned broadly at Miss Midgley and the Reverend Mr Soames as we tucked silently into our cereal and slightly burned toast.

I wanted to tell them, "I'm going to eat slightly burned toast for the rest of my life, because I'm head over heels in love again. But it won't be here in this Victorian villa with its stained-glass windows and mahogany sideboards, but in some tiny, tucked-away cottage in the country, with an acre or so of garden, and apple trees all pink petalled and beautiful in springtime.

"Miss French and I will raise puppies and kittens, and foster homeless children, and welcome our friends. We'll watch late-night films until our eyes boggle, because that's the way we will want it."

But I didn't say anything. I simply ate my breakfast, and then rushed out into the hall to kiss my very own Elizabeth.

"I have to go to the hairdresser's this morning, darling," she said, reaching up to smooth my hair and fix my tie. "Mind if I go with you on the bus?"

"I'd mind very much if you didn't, Liz," I said.

Then I watched, slightly stunned, as she took a scarlet umbrella from the hall-stand, stepped out into the rain, opened it, and twirled it as tantalisingly as one of those Southern belles in an old Hollywood musical.

"Liz," I said. "That umbrella. Where did you get it?"

"I bought it in the January sales." Her fine, fair eyebrows drew into a worried line. "Why do you ask?"

"Why did you buy it?" I just had to know.

She considered the question momentarily. Then she smiled up at me. "Because it made me feel . . . Oh, I don't know . . . rather — special and . . ."

"Beautiful," I said softly, remembering Janet. □

Complete Story by ROSEMARY ALEXANDER

A S the only member of our family who isn't terrified of Great-Aunt Gwen, I'm quite unique. She's either a born organiser or an insufferable busybody — according to the generosity and kindness of the person describing her!

She visits us for a fortnight, every summer.

"And that's quite sufficient!" Granny declares. "A little of Gwen always went a very long way. I couldn't call my soul my own, with that bossy creature around. We were all relieved when Henry qualified, and joined his father's practice in the North."

Aunt Gwen had met and married Uncle Henry while he was articled to a Twickenham solicitor. He's just the kind of gentle, submissive man who invariably falls victim to a strong-minded girl. At least, that was the popular view of their relationship.

That was how I saw it, too, until my holiday in Roxham.

The holiday was the result of a bug I'd contracted soon after I finished my college course. I was quite ill for nearly a month and, when I recovered, my mother insisted on a change of air.

"I'll phone Gwen," Granny said. She can be almost as bossy as her much-maligned elder sister. "If it's a change of air Judith needs, she won't find any more bracing than in Northumbria."

"You can't send me to Howton House!" I protested. "What on earth would I do there?"

"There *are* other amusements besides discos and coffee bars," my mother snapped. She must have been rather tired of having me drooping around the house like a withered daffodil.

"And they're healthier ones, too. Aunt Gwen may be in her eighties, but she still insists on plenty of exercise — which is just what you need, dear. She knows absolutely everyone for miles around, too. I guarantee you won't be bored."

I didn't think much of my mother's guarantees after a few days in Roxham. I was exhausted with trying to keep up with a shaggy-headed old lady and a couple of hyper-active Labradors by day, and I was bored during interminable evenings.

Even a good book didn't protect me from my aunt's accounts of "skullduggery" on the district council, the in-fighting at the Townswomen's Guild, and the problems she faced manipulating the committees of the half-dozen charities of which she was the chairman.

GREAT-AUNT GWEN'S TREASURE

There was no gold, no jewels — only a very precious insight into the heart of a dear member of the family.

GREAT-AUNT GWEN'S TREASURE

Uncle Henry had evolved his own method of coping. He still spent some hours every day at the office, and in his spare time he surrounded himself with geological specimens in his study. Years ago, he had taken refuge from local affairs by starting to write a learned treatise on rock formations — an effort likely to be ready for publication by about the year 2000!

Then a merciful providence prompted Aunt Gwen to set me tidying the boxroom. On reflection, providence probably had less to do with the decision than my aunt's exasperation with a listless and unresponsive guest!

I'm not anything like an efficient housewife. To my far-from-finicky eye, the boxroom didn't seem to need tidying. It was simply a matter of rearranging stacks of old lampshades, broken chairs, jam jars, odd lengths of carpet, and hideous, inherited relics.

But junk always has an irresistible fascination — I suppose it appeals to the childish longing to find hidden treasure. The boxroom at Howton House didn't really seem likely to conceal sacks bulging with gold, or chests full of jewels, but it did stir that latent yearning.

And much to my amazement, I eventually did unearth something special.

At first the shoebox stuffed with little, leather-backed, loose-leaf diaries didn't enthrall me. But the date on one of the earliest of them was fascinating.

After all, the nineteen-twenties must have been very different from the world I know. Aunt Gwen would be only 15 or 16. Granny a pig-tailed schoolgirl! So, with a certain amount of awe, I flicked through the pages.

It's not really rude to read old diaries, especially the kind filled with notes like "Dentist 2.30." "Write M . . ." "Collect skirt from cleaner." Whoever had kept this particular record had gone into a little more detail, but there's a limit to the amount you can cram into the space for each day.

Gwendoline Naylor — height 5 ft 4 in., next-of-kin, Mrs Naylor of the same address — certainly didn't indulge in the soul-searchings of an Elizabeth Fry, or the delicate poetry of a Dorothy Wordsworth. She was writing about the hectic incidents in the life of a bright, young suburban girl.

Wonderful fun at the office. C. brought in the balloons she'd saved from the Police Ball. Went mad chucking them around until Miss P. stormed in, and got one slap on the nose. Simply livid. Ticked me off good and properly. Threatened to tell Mr M. to sack the lot of us, if all we could do was behave like children.

Hilarious to think of Great-Aunt Gwen under the thumb of the office dictator! I knew she'd been considered terribly progressive to take a job after leaving school, but I'd imagined something decorous and ladylike. I certainly hadn't pictured hi-jinks with balloons, and severe tickings-off from indignant superiors at the office.

But the days hadn't been all nose-to-the-grindstone. Social activities had filled the weekends. *Dance at town hall. Met boy who's like toughened-up Nijinsky. Absolutely topping.*

Well, well! Had Uncle Henry known about this? Or hadn't he appeared on the scene, yet? The little leather-backed book was quite fascinating. I settled down on an ancient divan to enjoy the story which was slowly emerging.

"Midsummer Night's Dream" at Old Vic with Henry. He was around after all. *Those devoted ox-eyes make me want to behave outrageously just to shock him!*

Naughty Gwen! But I sympathised with her irritation — there are men who affect me in the same way, born doormats, just begging you to wipe your feet on them.

On Sunday, she said she'd strolled through the park with Carrie Bendell. Grannie had shown me photographs of Aunt Gwen's friend, a tiny blonde with a wickedly-attractive grin. I could picture them fairly accurately.

Ran into Nijinsky who insisted on walking with us. Real name Timothy Preston. Works on local rag. Tremendous fun — positively ached with laughter after half an hour in his company.

THE atmosphere of that long-ago winter's day filled the boxroom. You could sense all the thoughts that Gwen would not have put down, even if she'd had the space and time. Throughout January and February, T.P.'s presence made itself felt increasingly. Henry still got an occasional mention . . . usually rather terse.

Old Faithful dropped in. Left Mother to entertain him. C. arrived, and we went down to the river where T. was messing about in his boat. He suggested a dinner dance next Sat. He'll be up in town anyway, interviewing some film star. Arranged to meet at the Piccadilly.

I turned quickly to Saturday. This was really exciting. Sure enough, the budding romance went on. Gwen was almost expansive now.

T. had us in fits! Danced with me lots, but I was in a funny mood. Churned-up, edgy, but terribly happy. Snubbed H., and felt a beast when he looked hurt. C. teased him about me. I wish she wouldn't take it for granted we're made for each other.

As if they were my own friends I saw them . . . witty, scurrilous Timothy, Carrie a deliberate tease to poor, stolid Henry, and Gwen, uncertain how to deal with her feelings.

Dance at town hall. T. taught me to tango. Said I was poetry in motion!!!

That chap certainly knew how to chat up the girls — he never missed a cue.

Continued on page 86.

Say It With

Materials Required — Of **Madeira 6-strand Embroidery Cotton**, 1 skein each of Yellow 0104, Green 1306, Dark Purple 0714, Purple 0712, Lilac 0802.

10 x 10-centimetre, *4 x 4-inch,* piece of white Aida fabric, 14 blocks to 2.5 centimetres, *1 inch.*

Milward International Range tapestry needle No. 24.

White mounting card, 11 x 16 centimetres, *4¼ x 6¼ inches,* with an 8-centimetre, *3¼-inch,* circular aperture.

For best results it is essential to use the recommended materials. If you have difficulty in obtaining the materials, write direct, enclosing a stamped addressed envelope, to the following address for stockists: Madeira Threads (UK) Ltd., Customer Service Department, P.O. Box 6, Thirsk, North Yorkshire YO7 3YZ.

Identify each colour on the Key to Chart with its corresponding thread shade. You may prefer to whip around the raw edges of the fabric to prevent fraying.

Fold the fabric in half lengthwise and run a tacking thread along the fold. Repeat this widthwise. The point where the 2 tacking threads cross is your centre stitch.

Our beautiful pansy card makes a lovely keepsake. It is worked in counted cross stitch.

Flowers

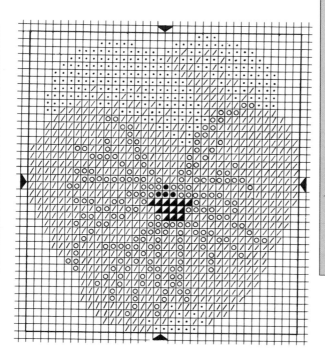

Identify and mark the centre stitch on your Chart. From this point the design can be counted according to the colours on the Chart. Each square on the Chart represents a complete cross stitch on the fabric.

When working cross stitch, take care that all the top threads are lying in the same direction.

This Madeira thread is made up of 6 strands; **use 2 strands throughout.**

When embroidery has been completed, press on the wrong side.

TO MAKE UP

On the wrong side of the card, make a square around the aperture using either double-sided tape or adhesive. Make sure the embroidery is centred in the aperture and stick down firmly. Again, using either double-sided tape or adhesive, stick the card backing flap over the back of the embroidery and stick firmly into position. ■

GREAT-AUNT GWEN'S TREASURE

Continued from page 83.

To the pictures. "Forbidden City." Sat next to T., and he held my hand. Certain he meant to suggest we go out without the others next time, but C. mentioned Elsie Ferguson, and T.'s got four free tickets for the Royalty, so that's that.

Then there were more tiny clues to what was starting to happen.

On bus to office, caught sight of C. talking to T. on steps of library. Miss P. furious when she came in late.

To town with Mother. Tea at Lyons Corner House. T. and Carrie there. They'd bumped into each other in the Strand. What a small world we live in!

The determinedly commonsense attitude was ominous. Pages of explanation couldn't have made the situation clearer. Abruptly, the happy dinner dances, the convivial foursomes, ended. The entries began to record more mundane incidents.

Altered hat. Washed hair. Helped Mother with tea cosies she's making for church bazaar. H. came round about seven.

And the following Saturday:

Fed up. Pictures with H. "Her Final Reckoning." Very apt, the way I feel.

How did she feel? It wasn't too hard to imagine.

Office dreary beyond words. Can't stand Miss P.'s nagging much longer.

Carrie seemed to have vanished completely, though her vivid personality still lingered.

Read stupid novel by Ruby M. Ayres. Went to bed early. H. called. Mother told him I had a headache.

There were even blank pages she hadn't bothered to fill in, spaces all the more poignant because of what wasn't written down. It was as if a light had been switched off, leaving a dark, deserted room.

Summer brought tennis parties, family picnics, a ramble over the Downs with Henry, but no mention of Carrie or that charmer, T.P. Not a word, not a single, significant abbreviation, showed they still existed. In September, after a supper with friends whose names I could not decipher, there was a curiously flat entry.

H. asked me to marry him. Said I would.

A DOOR crashed shut. The Labradors had begun the hysterical whimpering which meant Aunt Gwen was ready for their afternoon walk. I went downstairs to join her, and the sight of her sturdy, tweed-clad figure almost made me want to cry.

Nevertheless, I was still curious as we walked towards the moors above the town.

"What happened to your friend, Carrie Bendell?" I asked, as though making polite conversation. "Granny's always telling us stories about the crazy things you two got up to, when you were young."

At first, I thought she hadn't heard. Then Aunt Gwen bent down to unclasp the dogs' leads, and they raced ahead of us, barking frantically.

Straightening up, she looked at me.

"Carrie Bendell! Fancy Mary remembering her. I haven't seen her in over forty years."

"Did she leave Twickenham before you?"

From the photographs in the family album, I knew that Carrie hadn't been a bridesmaid at her wedding, and now the reason was plain.

"Yes. She married a reporter from the local paper, and they went up to Manchester when he got a job there. His name was Timothy Preston. Much later, during the Second World War, he became quite famous.

"He was killed in a Wellington bomber during a raid on Germany . . . not one of the crew, of course. He was too old for that. He'd gone with them as a war correspondent."

WE walked on behind the capering Labradors, and somehow I felt that Aunt Gwen knew I knew about that distant heartbreak. Her forthright, domineering manner had softened now into friendly silence.

I thought how sad it was that her work for good causes, her public life, had been a substitute for all she'd lost in that far-off springtime. The high-spirited girl who'd written the diary had died, and from her ashes had risen this rather aggressively cheerful woman.

"It must be fascinating to have so much to look back on," I said, when we paused for breath under the pine trees. "Life's so complicated . . . so full of dramas that seem the end of the world at the time."

"Fascinating!" Aunt Gwen can be drier than the Sahara, when emotion threatens. "If you're the kind of person who looks back . . . which I'm definitely not."

This effectively stopped any nostalgic reminiscences. But, as we started to retrace our steps, she added, almost inconsequentially, "You know, Judith, after all these years, Henry still thinks the world of me. He'd be lost without me . . . and I'd be lost without him."

Without any doubt, it was true. Like a strong tree and a luxuriant ivy, my aunt and uncle had grown together. With a new tenderness, I glanced at the fierce old lady.

A tear trickled down the furrows in the weatherbeaten cheek, but, in a flash, Aunt Gwen was her usual, brusque, indomitable self again.

"Buck up, Judith! A girl of your age certainly ought to put up a better performance. It's high time we were back indoors now. This wretched wind is making me cry." □

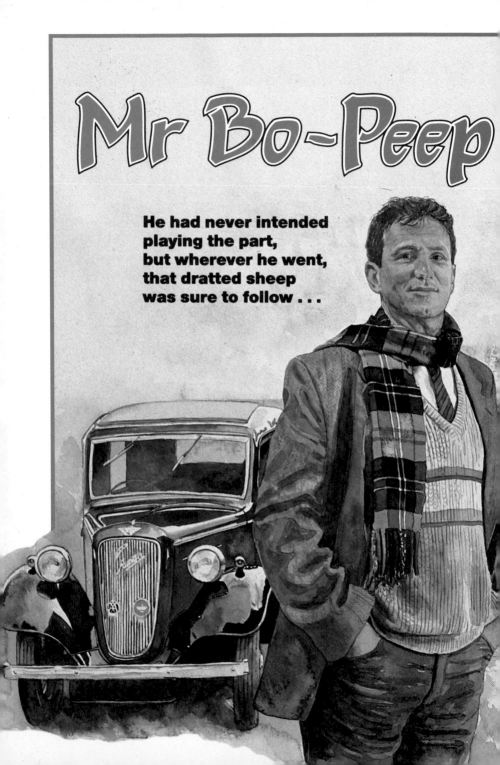

Mr Bo-Peep

He had never intended
playing the part,
but wherever he went,
that dratted sheep
was sure to follow . . .

Complete Story by D. L. GARRARD

"IT'S exactly what I was looking for, Mrs Burton," I said enthusiastically. "And in beautiful condition too."

The old lady smiled, gratified. "My husband always was handy, took a pride in his property."

Her eyes roved affectionately round the living-room of Jingle Cottage, which was chock-a-block with knick-knacks, polished brasses and burnished copper.

I could see she had a penchant for filling every available inch of space.

"I'll miss it, you know, when I move to my sister in town, even though the damp gets into my old bones. It's all that water so close, I expect.

"I've lived here all my married life, Mr Chase, and your first home is always special."

"It'll be my first home, too," I told her. "I've rented a bedsit up to now." I glanced round with a more critical eye. "I'd want to make some alterations, of course . . ."

MR BO-PEEP

Absently I rapped on the dividing wall with my knuckles, a habit I'd learned when testing for reasonably sound-proof accommodation. In some places I'd had, you could almost hear a mouse breathe through the paper-thin division.

But I realised there was no need to worry here — it was solid and would be all mine.

The tiny detached cottage, in full view of the reservoir, was as near to ideal as I'd hoped to find.

The bathroom and toilet were in a side extension and the first necessary improvement would be the building of a car-port on the other side to give some protection to my old banger.

This cluster of cottages and purpose-built houses for workers round Selham Water was fairly exposed to open country.

Downstairs, I decided, would do as my living quarters. They would be furnished simply, with none of the present clutter. Upstairs I'd turn the larger bedroom into a workroom and studio. With the light from the large dormer window it would be a perfect situation.

"As soon as I get back to Bonningford I'll go straight to the agent and clinch the deal, Mrs Burton," I told her.

She smiled and sighed. "It's not nice to think of your home being changed when you've gone, but I'm glad you're satisfied. I was beginning to think I wasn't going to get the price I need. People either want central heating and double glazing, or they expect to pay next to nothing.

"But there is just one thing . . ." She hesitated. "It's Sylvia. She'll have to go with the cottage, I'm afraid."

"Sylvia?"

"She's outside —" Mrs Burton began, but at that point a young woman entered without knocking.

I looked at her curiously. She wore jeans, boots and baggy sweater topped by an anorak, and her hair peeped brightly ginger from the rim of a cheerful-looking woolly hat.

"Oh, hello, dear," Mrs Burton interrupted herself. "This is Mr Chase, he's very interested in the cottage."

The girl gave me a thorough going over with penetrating green eyes. She had a long nose and rather pointed chin, and I wondered why on earth she had to go with the cottage.

Some sort of daily domestic, I supposed, which was the last thing I needed.

"Hello," the girl said. I noticed she spoke with as little enthusiasm as I was feeling.

"Hello, Sylvia," I responded, and was startled by a burst of laughter from Mrs Burton.

"Dear, oh, dear, that's my fault for not introducing you properly. This is June Ransome, she works at the fishing lodge. Oh, June, fancy being mistaken for . . ."

Mrs Burton spluttered, wiped her eyes, then beckoned me to the door. "No, Sylvia's outside. You must come and meet her, Mr Chase."

Puzzled, embarrassed, and aware that for some reason June Ransome hadn't entered into the mysterious joke nearly as thoroughly as Mrs Burton, I followed outside.

The cottage stood in a half acre of ground, mostly grass, and was surrounded by low, loose stone walls. Mrs Burton led me round to the side.

"Here's Sylvia," she announced.

S LIGHTLY stunned, I found myself gazing at a very hefty sheep, heavily clothed in shaggy grey wool. She bleated loudly on seeing Mrs Burton, but on catching sight of me fixed me suspiciously with sloe-black eyes.

"Dear old Sylvia," Mrs Burton said fondly, scratching her between the ears. "We found her one very bad winter after a blizzard, and in the end we kept her as a pet. She wouldn't mix with the flock now — she thinks she's a human being."

I couldn't see the resemblance myself, and Sylvia looked as if she was very doubtful about me.

Mrs Burton went on speaking.

"The trouble is, no-one's able to take her. She's been one of the family, really — I want her to finish her days here."

"But I don't know the first thing about animals," I protested quickly.

"She's no trouble, really. She's happy grazing on the half acre and I give her extra turnips. Once a year, Bill Colt shears and dips her with the rest — and that's all there is to it."

Slowly, I shook my head. "I'm really sorry, but I couldn't consider it. I'll have enough to do, without that."

After all, I'd decided to move mainly to gain more time and space. I was lucky enough to have developed my talent for drawing into a commercial proposition, but I wanted to do something more than illustrations.

There were masterpieces inside me waiting to get out, if only they had a real chance.

"Men do find it difficult to cope domestically," June Ransome said, rather disparagingly. "It'll probably take Mr Chase all his time to look after himself, let alone Sylvia.

"I'd accept the offer from the doctor's widow, if I were you, Mrs Burton," she finished. "What's a bit less money, if she's prepared to look after Sylvia?"

The thought of losing Jingle Cottage so soon after I'd found it jabbed me as much as June Ransome's appraising green eyes were doing.

Remembering how I'd been looking after myself since I left my foster home, I heard myself answer, "On reflection, I'm sure Sylvia and I will get along fine."

MR BO-PEEP

I ASKED my landlady's son, Steve, to help me move, since he owned a van. That way, I could drive down in my car and the whole operation would be over in one go. So, on a bright, sunny day, I led the way to Selham Water in my old car, Steve following behind.

I'd paid Mrs Burton for some basic furniture, and Steve's load mainly comprised my personal belongings as well as timber and rigid plastic with which I intended to put up a temporary shelter for the car.

I'd hopes of doing that during my first week, as settling into the cottage shouldn't take long.

I felt the thrill of ownership as I unlocked the front door, while Steve let down the tail of the van. We unloaded, and I was unearthing my electric kettle for some tea before Steve left, when I heard footsteps on the brick path.

Steve came clattering down the steep stairs which faced the front door.

"Hey!" he was shouting. "Did you know there was a sheep in your back garden? Oh, and a lady at the front door!"

It was June Ransome. "Mr Colt asked me to tell you he starts shearing a week on Monday. He'll do Sylvia as usual, if you bring her along."

"Thanks for letting me know." I waved the kettle. "Won't you stay and have a mug of tea with us?"

She stepped back, nervously. "No thanks."

"Wait a minute," I called as she turned away. "Where is the farm, and how do I get Sylvia there?"

"It's the other side of Selham Water — just follow the track round past the lodge." She waved a hand. "It takes you through the trees, past the bird-watching hides, and over the ridge. You'll see the farm then."

"It looks like a long walk."

She shrugged. "The road through Selham Village does run near the farm on the other side, but you'd really need a truck, or something bigger than your car."

She disappeared.

It took only a few days to get sorted out, but after Mrs Burton's clutter, my few belongings made Jingle Cottage seem bare. The furniture looked stark and the place somehow lacked warmth and homeliness.

I couldn't put my finger on just what was wrong, but it certainly wasn't quite as I'd visualised it.

My work-room was satisfactory, but I spent the rest of the week arranging and re-arranging with no better results.

Then, the following Monday, I had to take Sylvia for her shampoo and short-back-and-sides.

As Mrs Burton had said, she'd really been no trouble. She was perfectly quiet, and I'd hardly taken any notice of her apart from

supplying her daily turnips — which she actually didn't seem very keen on.

She never greeted me, only gave that suspicious stare which, strangely enough, unnerved me.

"Come along, Sylvia!" I said, with a heartiness which hid my trepidation. Or so I thought.

Perhaps Sylvia sensed it, for she made no response to heartiness, coaxing or downright irritability. Meanwhile, time was trickling away.

I stopped tugging at her and went round behind her.

"Time for walkies," I suggested impatiently, nudging Sylvia's posterior with my knees.

It was like trying to move Ben Nevis.

I tried again, and when I straightened up, perspiring and cross, I saw June Ransome watching me over the wall.

"Need a hand?" she enquired, politely.

At the sound of her voice Sylvia moved so fast that I fell to my knees on the wet grass.

"I needed a block and tackle till you appeared!" I shouted, above Sylvia's joyful bleating.

"Put her on the lead, she'll know what you want then," June suggested. "She's only a sheep, you know — she can't read your mind."

"Why not, if she's supposed to be so well trained?" I retorted rather stiffly.

"The lead's hanging on a peg in her shed. Actually, she doesn't like being sheared — it upsets her dignity — and she always needs some encouragement.

"I've got to go up to the farm myself," she finished. "I'll take her if you can't manage."

I'd have liked nothing better, but her attitude, for some reason, had provoked me again. "Far be it for me to shirk my duties," I said. "However, if you wouldn't mind coming along to allay Sylvia's phobias . . . ?"

After the shearing, Sylvia was delivered back to me, like a ghost of her former self. I buckled on her collar and lead, but though June had vanished somewhere among the farm buildings, Sylvia seemed anxious to get moving.

She trotted in front of me, her rolls of exposed fat quivering in the fresh breeze, plodding unerringly in the direction of Jingle Cottage.

Birds were singing everywhere, and the air was fresh. My good humour returned — after all, my duty was done for a year now, apart from the turnips.

I conducted Sylvia back to her quarters, almost tempted to scratch her forehead.

"There you are, old girl. Now, how about trying some of those turnips?" I told her.

Soon, however, I developed a new worry.

Sylvia still wasn't eating her turnips, and I hadn't noticed her grazing, either. I thought she looked thinner, but that could have been an illusion due to her shorn fleece.

After posting a batch of work on Friday, I took a walk along the shore.

Only when I arrived at the fishing lodge did I admit to myself why I'd come that way. Maybe I'd run into June, and casually ask her opinion about Sylvia. Just so the wretched sheep would stop interfering with my peace of mind.

A S I got nearer the lodge, June came out on to the veranda. She had discarded outdoor clothes and looked completely different in a fitting T-shirt dress with a silky scarf knotted at the neck.

I looked at her curiously as she stood, her hair being teased in the breeze and her skin glowing under the sun. She had a natural bloom such as I'd never noticed on a girl before.

"What's wrong — have I turned green or something?" June gave a rather uncertain laugh.

OUR QUICK CROSSWORD

Solutions To Crossword On Page 23.

"Sorry —" I began, but my stare was nothing to the one she then fixed on me.

"I wanted a word with you, Mr Chase — about Sylvia. She doesn't look very well."

"Agreed. I actually came to see if you could suggest anything," I said.

"Pets need attention," she said a little severely.

"If I'd wanted a pet, I'd have brought one with me. I certainly wouldn't have chosen a sheep — she was conditional on having the cottage. Remember?"

"Well, as you took on the responsibility, you should discharge it properly."

"You can lead a sheep to turnips, but you can't make it eat," I paraphrased in exasperation.

"And sheep don't live by turnips alone, not pet sheep anyway," she responded.

I sighed. "I honestly don't know anything about animals, so you owe it to Sylvia, if not to me, to come and make sure nothing's really wrong."

June called in on her way home. "I can't stay long. My front-lamp batteries are weak and I don't want to push the bike home." She gave me a faint smile.

Sylvia's welcoming bleat sounded dispirited. June talked to her soothingly, and presently Sylvia began to nibble a turnip tentatively, June fed her a whole one, piece by piece, while I watched with increasing dismay.

"Don't tell me I've got to do that!"

"It's not necessary normally . . . but I suppose you've just been throwing a turnip at her and ignoring her? She's pining for affection." She held a piece of turnip out to me. "Here — you try."

Sylvia turned her back.

June sighed and got to her feet.

"Well, I suppose I could drop in on my way home from work like I used to, and make sure she eats."

"But it isn't going to solve the problem, is it?" I asked. "Since Sylvia belongs to me, I really can't impose on you indefinitely."

"If we feed her together, she might eventually get the idea you belong around here, and accept the new order of things," she suggested.

"We can give it a try. I can't see any other way out," I said morosely.

FOUR days later, Sylvia stretched out her neck and nosed the piece of turnip I was offering her. Ridiculous as it was, I felt unexpectedly thrilled.

"Now scratch her between the ears," June ordered. "Make a fuss of her — as if you mean it!"

"Do you really think she knows or cares?"

"Of course she does! We've got a very unhappy, wounded ego on our hands."

Gingerly, I scratched.

"Come on, Sylvia. If you don't eat your turnips your wool won't curl," I encouraged.

June's mouth twitched and I held my breath. Suddenly her whole face melted into an enchanting mixture of mirth and mischief. Then, just as quickly, it hardened again.

"What are you going to do with that?" she asked. I followed her gaze to the stack of timber which had evidently escaped her notice until now.

"I need a garage, or something. More than I need a sheep, actually."

My joke fell flat.

"Where are you going to build it?" she asked.

"Just here."

"But this is Sylvia's favourite spot! Moving will make her unsettled again . . ."

"This is my cottage, you know." I tried to control my voice. "She'll have to adjust to circumstances — like I've had to! Or, of course, there's the alternative. I could get rid of . . ."

"The car," I was going to say, but the sarcastic impulse died and my voice tailed off.

I was noticing all kinds of things about June which I'd never seen until now. There was the powdering of freckles which would probably flower in profusion in the summer . . . the soft shape of her mouth . . .

June stood up abruptly. "Tell me if Sylvia needs me again," she said.

"June . . ."

She seemed not to hear and I didn't call after her. I wasn't sure what I'd been about to say. I'd never been at a loss with a girl before, but June was a new kettle of fish.

"Back to the drawing board!" I ordered myself crossly. I hadn't enough time for Sylvia, let alone June as well.

I began on my first canvas with determination, but every time I paused, a vision of June's urchin face flashed before my eyes. I worked doggedly through the following week but by Friday I was forced to admit that the situation was definitely interfering with my work.

I even found myself talking to Sylvia about it — sometimes she actually seemed to listen.

I tried to face the problem squarely. Did June really dislike me, and if so was there any particular reason? There was something about June Ransome, despite her apparent hostility, which affected me in a way no-one else ever had.

I had to bring it to a head. It was just about time for June to come by on her bicycle, and the only way to find out the truth of the matter was to ask. I had a feeling that honesty would be one of her strong points.

I went to the window with my mug of tea just in time to see a shiny new Range-Rover pull up outside. After a moment I recognised it as belonging to Liz's father, and sure enough Liz was climbing out of it, in a white trouser-suit.

Liz worked as a secretary and receptionist with the publishing firm I did my illustrations for. She and I had had a rather tempestuous and stormy relationship for nearly a year, but we'd eventually decided, amicably, that we weren't right for each other. Our lifestyles were too different.

So, with no trouble at all, we'd transformed our relationship into one of easy friendship.

Now, as I stood taken aback by her unexpected arrival, I caught a glimpse of June approaching on her bicycle.

Then everything seemed to happen at once.

As Liz stepped gingerly on to the crooked brick path, Sylvia came galloping round the side of the cottage, emitting her usual June greeting.

Seeing the sheep charging in her direction, Liz let out a wild shriek.

I dashed to fling open the door and Liz fell against me.

"Geoff!" she gabbled hysterically. "Save me! Get that monster away!"

Over her shoulder I saw June assess the situation and ride on, leaving Sylvia bleating woefully after her.

I unwound Liz from round my neck.

"Calm down. Sylvia's quite tame, and she wasn't interested in you, anyway."

"Sylvia?" Liz straightened her jacket and grabbed at her dignity. "You must be at your wits' end if you've started keeping sheep for company."

"Come on in," I invited. "And tell me why you're here."

"Well, there was an important agreement for you to sign, and I had the afternoon off, so I said I'd bring it down to you. I felt like a change, anyway . . .

"Oh, Geoff, is tea all you can offer me?"

"Yes. But I'll take you to the Pig and Whistle when they open. They do a nice line in basic food, too."

"That's nice, but I mustn't be late back. Going out with Mark tonight," Liz said airily.

"The Pig and Whistle's on your way. We'll go early in the Range-Rover, then I'll stay on after you for a pint or two and walk home. That way I get to know people."

WHEN Liz had departed after a meal and half an hour's basking in admiring glances, someone I recognised from the Selham Water estate came up to me. I wondered why he was grinning.

"There's someone outside looking for you."

I hurried out, hoping it wasn't Liz returning after some mishap, and quelling the irrational idea that by some strange telepathy June had come searching for me to make her peace.

It wasn't either.

"Maa-aaa!" Sylvia said, speaking unmistakably to me for the first time in our lives. She sounded thoroughly bored and impatient.

"What's the matter with you?" I enquired, stupidly.

She came and leaned on my legs.

"Get away!" I protested, tottering sideways, but oddly flattered all the same.

We ambled homewards along the shadowed lane, Sylvia zig-zagging in front of me. There was no moon yet, only starlight, and I kept bumping into her as she stopped to investigate things. I became so intent on not falling over her that I was paying no attention to the road.

Then, rounding a bend, I came face to face with a dim, wavering light, and a dimmer form astride a bicycle behind it.

Sylvia bleated joyfully. The next thing I knew, the bicycle, June and myself were in a heap with Sylvia trampling all over us.

"Sylvia! Thank goodness!" June cried, with a surprising catch in her voice.

"June!" I cried, at exactly the same time. "Are you all right?"

I helped her up. She was warm and light, and her soft, springy hair smelled faintly of shampoo.

"What on earth were you doing? Taking Sylvia for a walk?"

"I took Liz to the pub and she followed me. June, you're crying! Are you hurt?"

"Only a bruise or two, I've fallen off a bike before," she said huskily.

"Then what's the matter?" I asked gently.

June wiped her eyes. "I had to go back to the lodge for

something," she said. "I thought I'd say hello to Sylvia if there was no-one around, only she wasn't there. She was a nuisance to you, so I thought frightening your girlfriend must have been the last straw.

"You said there was one alternative . . . I thought you'd taken her away in the Range-Rover to get rid of her." She gulped.

"Tell me, June, is Sylvia the reason you've always been at loggerheads with me?"

She shook her head.

Encouraged by the fact that she hadn't shrugged my hands from her shoulders, I pressed on gently. "Then why, June? Please tell me. It matters."

"So does Jingle Cottage, to me." She gave a shuddering sigh. "It was my real home, even before Dad died. Mrs Burton was a second mother to me. But I knew she was getting desperate to sell, and I guessed you only needed the right sort of push to take up a challenge.

"But then she told me you were going to knock down walls and change everything. I know it's nothing to do with me, yet in a way it is, so much. It was like waiting to see someone you love undergo a . . . a calamitous operation!"

I laughed aloud with relief. "I'm building nothing, except that garage."

I said carefully, "Liz and I are just friends. She brought something for me to sign."

Encouraged by her silence, I went on.

"Perhaps you could advise me on what Jingle Cottage needs to turn it from a house into a home?"

"What —?" she began, but the explanation of that was delayed by our first kiss.

It didn't last more than two shakes of a lamb's tail because Sylvia felt left out and came to lean on us.

But I didn't mind — I knew we'd all the time in the world ahead of us. □

Complete Story by SARAH BURKHILL

Every Second Saturday

**The time he spent with his daughter
was short — but, oh, so precious. And
the years would never dim the
happiness they'd shared . . .**

IT'S almost three days now since I last saw you, Ruth. I hope
you didn't miss tea on Saturday, and the chocolate gateau
your mum was baking. It was too bad, us getting held up
in all that traffic from the football match. My fault, of course. I
should have been taking you home earlier, but those last few
minutes were so precious and I kept delaying the moment when
I would have to let you go.

Every second Saturday . . . It's not much time for a man to
spend with his daughter, is it? Once I tried to calculate just how
many hours we have been together in these last six years. It
worked out at about 780.

It's not a long time. Just over a month, if you ran all the
hours together.

One month . . . I suppose at your age that seems endless.

Especially this coming month, the last one you will spend on this island of ours.

Already you are in almost a frenzy of excitement, talking non-stop about America and what life will be like in that vast country you have been hearing about these past three years.

Oh, Ruthie, where do I begin? There is so much you should know, so much I want you to understand before you leave.

The difficulty of my decision to let you go. The agony of signing the paper which would take away all those rights the court awarded me six years ago.

And then this last thing, the hardest of all . . .

BUT that's not the beginning of it, Ruth. The beginning of it was 14 years ago, when your mother and I walked into a church and vowed before God that we would love each other for ever.

Does that seem a funny kind of promise to make? Perhaps to you it doesn't, everything being clear-cut and simple in your 12-year-old mind.

And to us, too, everything was clear-cut and simple, at first.

We were lucky, your mum and I. Not for us the poky little furnished flat. I was beginning to do well in my job and we bought a nice two-bedroomed house over at King's Abbey.

Having to be away a lot on business was a bit of a bore, but even that didn't matter. Often your mother would come with me, and on our long drives across the country we would talk of the day when that second bedroom, our spare room, would have a permanent occupant.

Two years later, it did. It's a funny thing, Ruth, but up until the moment you were born I had been longing for a son.

When the nurse came out to tell me Adele had given birth to a daughter, I didn't quite believe it for a minute. I just sat and stared at her, until suddenly I felt this rush of — what? Emotion, joy, all-consuming wonder? I can't explain it really.

I just knew, all at once, that having a little girl was the best thing that could possibly happen to anyone.

A while later, when the chap waiting with me learned that his wife had been delivered of a boy, I said, "Shame!"

I was so sorry for him, so full of commiseration that he had been denied the marvellous experience that was mine.

It was your mother who chose the name Ruth.

I looked it up in our dictionary of names: "Meaning is obscure" it said, "Possibly associated with the English word for sorrow or misfortune."

Sorrow. There's nothing sorrowful about you, is there, Ruthie? You're happy, healthy, well-adjusted — remarkably well-adjusted in the circumstances.

We were happy, too, in those first months after you were born.

It's difficult to remember just when things started to go wrong.

Perhaps it was on your first birthday when I was delayed in Birmingham, and couldn't get home for the cutting of the cake. Maybe not. Perhaps that was only the first time your mother actually said anything about my being away so much.

After that, it started to get worse. Soon, even the time I spent at home was marred by quarrels or, worse, a strained, uncomfortable wall of silence.

It was just before your third birthday that we had our last row, though I didn't know then that it was the last.

I flew up to Inverness that afternoon, and — well, there was a girl there, Ruth. She was sitting in the hotel lounge, waiting for a friend who didn't show up. She was a nice girl, friendly and good humoured, and I took her out for a drink.

By the time we returned to the hotel it was after 10, and your mother was pacing up and down in the foyer.

Don't ask me why she had chosen that one night to come after me. Maybe she had sensed something in that final row that I hadn't seen, and was making one desperate attempt to recapture our earlier happiness.

But whatever the reason, she had got a baby-sitter for you and had followed me across half of Britain.

Of course she wouldn't believe that girl was a harmless, spur-of-the-moment happening. Maybe she didn't want to believe it.

When I got home from that trip, the house was empty. She had taken you to her mother's, and when I finally realised she wasn't coming back I moved out, too, gave her the keys, and . . . and that was the end of it, more or less.

"Just one of those things." That's the excuse people make these days, for everything and anything, and it's too easy.

All the same, there can sometimes be truth in it. Was it my work that broke up our marriage? Or a girl whose name I can't even remember? Or perhaps your mother's inability to cope with an unsettled life and long spells of being on her own?

Would things have been different if I'd had a job that kept me at home? Or was there some basic flaw in our relationship that would have made it impossible for us to overcome any difficulties at all?

I don't know, Ruth. Perhaps it really was "just one of those things."

And so life went on. It does that, Ruth. Don't ever believe what people tell you about the world coming to an end. That doesn't happen. There's still shopping to buy, food to cook, and work to be done — no matter what might have occurred.

And for me there was something else, too. There was every second Saturday.

What did we do in those 780 hours we spent together, I wonder now. Sometimes we went to the park, or to the zoo, but we couldn't have spent all those hours looking at animals or playing on swings.

EVERY SECOND SATURDAY

I suppose most of our time was spent talking — getting to know each other as you grew from babyhood and became a proper little person.

That wasn't easy in just two afternoons a month, but even then I learned things about you, the things that matter.

That you were alert and intelligent . . .

"School's boring," you told me when you were five. "All they ever do is play. I want to learn things properly!"

That you had plenty of friends.

"Jane and Carol asked me to a party this afternoon, but Mum said I couldn't go because you . . . because . . . she didn't want me to."

And that you were careful of others' feelings. You would never let me know that I had deprived you of a treat.

It must have been about three years ago that Andy started creeping into your conversation.

Andy brought you a book when he came to dinner last week. Andy took Mum and you to the cinema.

I didn't think much about it until the day you rushed to greet me and tell me that he and your mother were getting married.

Andrew Lomax was an American working in Britain, and oh, how I hated him the first and only time we met! Shiny black hair and gold-rimmed glasses. The all-American nice guy.

That's not fair, I know, Ruth! Andy is a nice guy, and when I could think more rationally I was glad you were to have him as a stepfather.

You were glad, too, and a few weeks after the wedding, your talk was of nothing but your new family.

"You should see the house we're living in now," you told me once when we met at my flat during the winter. "It's got a huge, big attic, and Daddy . . . I mean Uncle says . . ." You faltered, your face growing anxious.

"What does he say?" I asked, turning to look out of the window so you wouldn't see the pain you had caused. How sensitive you are, darling! How you hated to hurt this poor old guy who kept intruding in your life!

It didn't matter anyway, I knew you called him Dad. Your mother told me — not out of cruelty, but to reassure me that you were loved and happy.

Not that I needed any assurance. Your happiness was obvious, especially that day you told me you were getting a brother or sister.

"Which would you like, Ruth?" I asked.

"I don't know." You considered the matter . . . "A sister, I think. We're going to call her Pamela if it's a girl, only she'll be Pamela Lomax like Mum and . . . Uncle Andy. Not Armstrong like me."

"Congratulations," I told your mother when I took you home.

Normally I just leave you at the gate, but this time your mother was waiting in the garden, and she came over to the car.

"Thanks, Martin," she said and waved you inside.

"Martin, can I talk to you about Ruth?"

I didn't quite understand at first when she told me. What is Andrew's firm wanting him in New Jersey to do with me? What had it to do with my daughter?

Even when that sank in, I was still confused. How could they possibly take you over there? They couldn't expect me to commute twice-monthly to America, could they?

No, of course they couldn't. That was the point.

"It would be good for her, Martin," your mother said. "She'll have everything. She'll be happy, I promise you.

"But if you don't agree, well . . ." She shrugged. "I'll understand."

Yes, I think she would have understood.

B UT would you, Ruth? After you overheard them talking about the proposed move, would you have forgiven me for spoiling it all?

"You mustn't tell anyone 'cause it's a secret and I'm not supposed to know," you whispered on our next Saturday out. "But — but we might be going to America!"

"Would you like that, Ruthie?" I asked.

"Oh, it would be marvellous!"

You dragged out my old atlas and began to point out the place.

"Look, that's it. Da — Uncle Andy's got a sister over there, and she'll be my auntie, and I've got masses and masses of cousins, and a grandpa and grandma — only, she doesn't look like a grandma, 'cause she wears slacks and she's got blue hair. I've seen pictures."

You sighed. "Oh, I do hope I can go."

"Don't worry, pet," I told you. "I bet you two kisses everything will work out just fine!"

Your mother was silent for a moment when I told her I would relinquish my access rights. Then she bent forward and kissed me briefly on the cheek.

"Thank you, Martin. I know . . ." She broke off and stared sadly at me before turning away. "Martin, I want to ask you . . ."

"What?" I said.

She twisted the wedding ring round on her finger and I noticed the tension in her face. "Andrew wants to legally adopt Ruth," she said eventually with a bluntness that took me aback. "He loves her, Martin. And she . . .

"Well, would you think about it? Please? You can give me your answer when we go to the lawyers next week."

So that's it, Ruthie. The whole story of these last years.

Well, no, not really the *whole* story. There's a few things I've missed out, things that don't concern you very much.

Jackie, for instance.

It was Jackie who made that rag doll I gave you for Christmas last year.

That was good of her, I thought, seeing we had only known each other for a few months.

But then she's a nice person. At her flat last night, when I ranted and raved to her over your mother's latest proposition, Jackie just sat quietly and gazed at me with sad, brown eyes.

"It's your decision, Martin. You'll do what you think best for Ruth."

Then she held me in her arms and the words repeated themselves over and over again in my head.

Best for Ruth. What's best for Ruth.

They are still echoing now, as I make my way to the lawyer's office where I will have to make that final, irrevocable decision. Does Andrew Lomax really love you, I wonder.

Yes, yes, he does. Knowing you, how could he do otherwise?

I cross the road and glance at my watch. I am early. There is still time to think.

There's a jeweller's shop on the corner of the street, and I stop to gaze in the window. I was here two weeks ago, looking at engagement rings, but now isn't the time for that and my eyes pass over them to the little gold bangles in the corner.

That would be a nice going-away present for you, Ruth. I'll go in and choose one.

"Do you want it engraved?" the man asks when I have made my selection.

"Yes. yes, that would be nice," I tell him, turning the bangle over in my hands. "Put . . . put to R . . . to R.L. from . . . Martin, with love."

That will be the best thing for you, Ruthie. Now you can have the same name as the rest of your family. Now Andrew can be legally what he has been in all but name for the last two years — your father.

You have his name now, Ruth. You will live in his home, and have his people as your people.

But you have my love, Ruth. Not just every second Saturday, but for ever.

Maybe Ruth was a fitting name for you after all. Wasn't there a Ruth in the Bible, who travelled to a foreign land and was loved and happy there amongst the people she chose as her family?

May you be happy with yours, my darling — and with the blessings I send with you. □

Complete
Story by
BETTY
HAWORTH

**From now on
she would simply
be herself.
It wasn't a hard
decision to make,
but keeping to it
was quite a
different matter.**

O N the morning of her 50th
birthday, Anna Fraser
got up and looked at
herself searchingly in her dressing-
table mirror.

"You're middle aged, Mrs
Fraser," she told herself. "You've
been middle aged for some time,
and now you have to admit it."

TURNING POINT

TURNING POINT

She leaned forward and looked critically at her own face in the mirror.

Yes, today was the day for her to make a decision, one that she had put off many times.

The trouble about getting older, Anna had discovered, was that the outside of you changed but the inside stayed more or less the same.

Anna still felt quite young inside — about 25, in fact — but whenever she caught sight of herself these days in a shop window or a mirror she got rather a surprise.

She had begun to avoid looking at her own reflection in windows recently, because she had noticed something about herself.

She wasn't sure exactly what it was. Her figure was still trim and she prided herself that she still weighed the same as when she had married at 19.

"Not many women of my age can say *that!*" she would tell herself in her desperate moments.

She had always looked after her skin, and the only little treat she allowed herself was blonde highlights in her hair when she had it washed and set by the hairdresser.

It brightened her appearance and made her look much younger . . . at least, that's what she'd always thought.

"Do all women feel like this when they reach their fiftieth birthday?" Anna asked the woman in the mirror. "Do they get up and realise that they have reached a turning point — a day of decision? Do they resent it like me — or do they accept it?"

How can I accept it, Anna thought bleakly. I don't believe any woman who says she doesn't care about growing old. Men seem to grow more attractive as they get older but for women it's different. For a woman, growing into middle age takes courage.

She opened the little drawer in the dressing-table and looked at the jars and bottles inside. They were wonderful things to improve her skin and hair, all very good in their way, but she knew that none of them contained any magical ingredient that would restore her youthful appearance.

Those belonged only in fairy stories.

The house was very quiet. Phil had gone to the office. There was a card for her stuck in the wall calendar. *Happy Birthday, Darling! Will be home early to celebrate,* he had written.

Dear Phil! He always took her out to dinner on her birthday to their favourite restaurant.

Even when the children were small and they were hard up, he had managed to take her out for a celebration meal or sometimes to the theatre.

As she made herself toast and coffee in the kitchen, she remembered all the birthdays they had spent together.

On her first birthday after they were married they had gone to London and queued for hours for a concert, eating sandwiches and chocolate. What happy times those were and how she sometimes longed to do something silly and impulsive like that again!

"That's what I mean about middle age," she said aloud. "I still feel young inside, but if I do anything impetuous or slightly crazy, people look at me as though I ought to know better."

A TAP on the kitchen door startled her and she turned to see a cheerful face smiling at her from the doorway. "Good morning, Mrs Fraser! Happy birthday!"

"Judy!" Anna cried, jumping up. "Come in! You're just in time for coffee!"

"Sorry!" Judy Powers came into the kitchen breathlessly and put the plant she carried down on the table. "I can only stay for a second. I've a million things to do. I just wanted to give you this plant."

"How kind!" Anna said, smiling at her young neighbour. "I'd just decided that this is going to be my last official birthday!"

"It's only one of my Busy Lizzie plants." Judy laughed. "But it has masses of red flowers and I thought it would cheer you up!"

"Did you?" Anna replied lightly. "Do I look as if I need cheering up then?"

"No, I didn't mean . . ." Judy blushed and laughed again. "I just thought you'd been looking a bit tired lately."

Very tactful, Anna thought ruefully. So she's noticed something too!

"I'm fifty today," she said, and saw the expression of faint embarrassment on the girl's face.

"Honestly, Mrs Fraser? Well, you certainly don't look it! I must dash now or I'll miss my bus!"

She doesn't understand, Anna thought, smiling. She hasn't the slightest inkling of what it means to be 50.

"Thank you for the plant," she said. "It was a kind thought."

"You're welcome. Sorry I've got to rush off, but I'll be late for work if I don't!"

"Judy," Anna said as she turned to go. "I know you're busy with your job and the house to look after, but you'll try not to rush about too much, won't you?"

"Oh, I'm all right!" Judy laughed, tossing back her mop of dark hair. "Just badly organised, that's all!"

"Life's very short," Anna said. "You don't want to wake up one day and find you've rushed it all away, do you?"

Judy gave her a surprised look and a moment later she had hurried off.

That was rather pompous, Anna thought. Just because she's young and full of energy. You'll have to hide your feelings better than that, Mrs Fraser!

There were several letters on the mat in the hall, bills and circulars, and with them a card from Sally with a picture of a rabbit in cricket gear and something silly inside about knocking up a half-century.

Anna stood with the card in her hand and felt a flush of anger run through her.

Surprise followed quickly. Now why should she be annoyed at the card? It was only Sally's sense of humour — nothing to be upset about. She hadn't meant anything by it.

THE telephone rang on the hall table and she lifted the receiver on a babble of children's voices. Sally sounded harassed.

"Hello, Mum! Happy birthday."

"Hello, dear! Thanks for the card. I've just opened it."

"Hang on a sec," Sally said and there was more noise and howls of protest dying away in the distance.

"What d'you think?" Sally asked, returning to the phone. "Danny's got chickenpox and that means the twins will get it at any minute, and I've got the decorator coming tomorrow to paper the lounge."

"Oh, Sally, I am sorry," Anna said. She hesitated and there was a brief silence.

"Who'd be a mother!" Sally sighed. "Oh well, not to worry. Are you dining out tonight?"

"Yes, my birthday treat," Anna said.

"Lovely!" Sally said. "Danny's making you a card. It might not be finished for a long time."

"Give him my love," Anna told her. "And the twins, too. When will we see you all again?"

"Goodness knows." Sally laughed. "The weeks rush by and I never have time to turn round. How long does chickenpox last?"

"I've forgotten," Anna said.

"Oh well, never mind. I'll give you a ring when they're all better. Must fly now, darling! Love to Dad! Look after yourself . . . 'Bye!"

Anna put down the phone and caught sight of herself in the hall mirror.

"You're getting selfish, too," she told herself.

She could have offered to go and help Sally for a few days. Phil wouldn't have minded, but suddenly the prospect of coping with three noisy, energetic children had made her shudder.

At lunch-time another card came for her with a letter, and Anna sat down with her lunch on a tray to read it. John never forgot his mother's birthday and his card, all the way from Canada, always reached her on the right day.

The letter was full of news of John and his family. When she had finished reading, the house seemed very silent and strangely lonely. John's birthday card had red roses and a beautiful verse that brought tears to Anna's eyes.

O VER lunch she thought about John and wished once again that he wasn't working so far away. He had been a mischievous and demanding little boy — rather like Sally's Danny — and Anna thought regretfully about his childhood years that she had spent rushing around doing things that could have been left and worrying about things that weren't really important.

If only she could have those precious years back again, knowing what she knew now.

At two o'clock Anna went into town to have her hair done.

Why was it that today the small salon where she went seemed full of smart young women?

The girl in the next chair had shining brown hair, and she was looking at herself closely in the big round mirror in front of her, turning her head this way and that to examine her freshly-cut hair. She caught Anna's eye and smiled, a young, confident smile, as she got up to go.

"Hello, Mrs Fraser!" the assistant greeted her cheerfully. "Rinse, wash and set as usual?"

Anna took a deep breath. "No." She smiled at the girl via the mirror. "Just a wash and set this time, please. I've decided not to have it rinsed any more."

The girl put her head on one side consideringly.

"I'm bowing to the inevitable." Anna laughed.

"Are you sure? It won't look the same."

"Quite sure," Anna said firmly. "And can you cut it for me, please? I feel I need a new style."

"You *are* making changes!" The girl smiled, but she still looked a little doubtful. "You're sure about the colour? There's quite a lot of grey in your hair . . ."

"That's hardly surprising, is it?" Anna replied lightly. "It's my fiftieth birthday today!"

The girl was embarrassed. She looked just as Judy had looked that morning in the kitchen, Anna thought.

"Happy birthday!" she said, reaching for her scissors.

Not as tactful as young Judy, Anna thought. Or perhaps not as kind.

Just over an hour later Anna was looking into the mirror again. The woman who looked back at her had short, curling hair, soft and prettily styled, but quite grey.

TURNING POINT

It was a mistake, Anna thought, struggling with tears. What on earth was I thinking of? I could have left it a bit longer, and it's too late to do anything about it today.

She went and had a cup of coffee.

Well, she'd done what she'd decided to do, and that was that! It was quite ridiculous to sit here feeling as though the end of the world had come!

It's a pity you haven't anything more important to worry about! she told herself angrily.

But still that feeling of desolation refused to leave her. She had taken a deliberate step today and she knew in her heart that she would not turn back.

THE little boutique in the High Street had a window full of bright dresses that made her feel better just looking at them. Inside there were masses of pretty things, dozens of dresses in every colour, and music playing as she looked around.

At the end of a long rack filled with trousers and sparkly evening tops she came upon a full-length mirror, and a slim, middle-aged woman in a navy suit. Anna stared for several seconds, then turned and walked out of the shop.

She walked along the main street until she reached the corner and turned into a quieter street. A little way down was a dress shop she had looked into occasionally but never been in to, because everything in the small window was so obviously expensive.

Once she had pointed out a dress to Sally, but Sally had laughed and said, "Good heavens, Mother, you can't go in there! I bet it's one of those shops you can't get out of . . . and look at the colours! Even if you are a granny, I don't want you to look like one!"

The window dressing was exquisite and in the centre was a white dress in silk that looked as though it cost a fortune.

Anna stood very close to the window, her nose almost touching the glass, and a longing came over her for a dress like that; something soft and beautifully cut and wickedly expensive.

Not really expensive, she thought. A dress like that is a joy for years.

Almost before she knew it, Anna was inside the shop. It was very quiet. She walked across the thick carpet and admired the arrangements of real flowers. It even smelt expensive!

Anna felt herself go hot and was on the point of turning back when a woman in a black dress came down the shop towards her and looked at her inquiringly.

"Good afternoon," Anna said nervously. "I'm looking for a dinner dress."

Even as she said the words, she felt surprised. It was an expression she hadn't used for years. Whoever talked about dinner dresses these days?

"A dinner dress," the woman said, smiling. "Had you any particular colour in mind?"

She had a quiet, friendly manner and Anna glanced at the rack of dresses nearby with a sudden feeling of excited anticipation.

The rack had a grey silk cover laid over it and only the hems of the dresses were showing. The woman pulled back the cover with a delicious swishing sound. The expensive scent grew stronger as the dresses were uncovered, not squashed tightly together but each one swinging gently on its padded hanger.

"I don't really mind about the colour," Anna said breathlessly. If the prices were too horrendous she could always pretend there was nothing she liked and escape that way!

The woman began looking carefully through the dresses although she hadn't asked Anna's size.

A good saleswoman doesn't need to ask, Anna thought. But I thought they were all extinct!

"Do you wear green?" She was holding up a dress for Anna to see.

"Not often. I don't like . . ." Anna's voice trailed away. The dress was green, a whisper of a dress in some silky material, soft as a cloud. She had had a dress almost like it when she got married and Phil had loved it.

"Would you like to try it on?"

It fitted like a dream, slightly clinging. The colour lit up her skin and made her feel like a million dollars. Anna knew that this was her dress.

"It's lovely," the woman said. "And you have the figure for it. Is it for a special occasion?"

"My husband is taking me out to dinner," Anna said quietly, staring at herself in the long mirror. "It's my fiftieth birthday."

The words sounded quite different now. The woman studied her for a moment, smiling.

"The perfect age," she said, laughing a little. "When a woman knows exactly what she can wear and how to wear it!"

It wasn't just sales talk; the mirror told Anna she was right. The green dress was tenderly folded into tissue paper and put into a dress box.

"Many happy returns," the woman said. "Have a lovely evening!"

When Phil came home, Anna was ready.

"I like the dress," he said at once. "Didn't you have one that colour a year or two ago?"

"A year or two," Anna said, kissing him.

"It's nice," he said, looking at her with an expression that made her heart turn over. "Suits you."

"Have you noticed anything else?" Anna asked, lifting her chin slightly.

He continued to look at her without answering.

"My hair," she prompted. "I decided to — "

H

"Have it cut," he interrupted, smiling. "I thought there was something different."

THEY dined quietly, and afterwards danced cheek to cheek, not saying very much. When the evening was nearly over, Anna said, "Sally rang up this morning. Danny's got chickenpox and the decorator's coming tomorrow."

"That's bad organisation," Phil said.

"I think she wanted me to go over and help out," Anna said. "She didn't ask outright and now I feel terribly guilty because I didn't offer to go. Do you think I ought to?"

"Anna," Phil said quietly, "Sally's a very capable young woman and I'm sure she can cope with her domestic crisis on her own this time. I think you ought to stay at home and just fuss over me instead."

"But, Phil," Anna said in surprise, "I am her mother."

"Yes," he said. "And you've done your share of coping. They're Sally's children, and she can manage them."

"But that's selfish!" she said.

"I know," he said. "One of the compensations of middle age."

"There aren't many, are there?" she asked suddenly, looking down at her plate.

"Oh, I don't know," he said. "It depends how you look at it. Looking at you in that green dress makes me think there are quite a lot."

She blushed, feeling the warmth stealing into her heart.

"It was horribly expensive," she said.

"Never mind," he said. "I've known my bank manager for a long time."

He reached across the table and took her hand. "Of course if you want to go to Sally's and wash nappies and wipe soggy cereal off the walls . . ."

She made a little sound, half laugh, half sob. "Phil, I'm fifty and my hair is going grey. I know you're being kind and pretending not to notice."

"So what?" he said. "So is mine!"

She looked up at him, smiling at her across the table. She felt a warm contentment that she hadn't felt for months.

"When I was eighteen," she told him, "I used to drool over men like you, Philip Fraser. Tall, middle-aged men with greying hair and lean, experienced faces."

"There you are then," he said. "You've had to wait a bit, but you've got what you wanted, haven't you? I told you, there are plenty of compensations for middle age. If I were rich, too, it would be perfect, but you can't have everything."

"I have everything I want," Anna told him from her heart. "This morning I was depressed because I seemed to realise all at once that

I wasn't young any more. Now it doesn't really matter."

"No, it doesn't really matter," Phil said, squeezing her hand. "If a person stays young inside, what happens to the outside isn't really important, is it?"

"Don't sound so smug," Anna said. "It's all right for you sitting there looking grey and distinguished and pretending not to notice all the eighteen-year-olds drooling!"

She was making a joke about it but he saw the shine of tears in her eyes and realised in that moment what this birthday meant to her.

A man can never completely understand a woman's heart, even a woman he has been married to for many years, but Philip Fraser understood in that moment just a little of what his wife was feeling.

He had noticed the changes, too, and been conscious of her restlessness these last months. Now he knew the reason.

HE stood up, taking her hand and leading her out on to the little dance floor.

They danced without speaking, holding each other close in sweet familiarity. When the music finished they stood and smiled at each other.

"Would you like another drink?" he asked.

"No, I don't think so," she said.

"If we go home now," he said, "we can put our feet up and watch the late-night film."

Anna sighed deeply. "Oh, let's do that, Phil," she said. "I'm dying to get these shoes off!"

"How romantic!" He laughed.

Anna laughed, too, and took his arm. It had been a lovely, memorable birthday after all, and her day of decision had not been as hard as she had expected.

Phil was right, there were compensations for middle age. A serenity that made one realise what a waste of time it was to fret and worry over unimportant things, and an ability to savour happy moments, to appreciate one's friends, to remember mistakes and not make them again.

Now, she could look back with laughter, and forward with confidence.

She smiled. The best years were still to come. □

A LESSON FOR LIVING

**The children were noisy
and unruly — but they taught
one lonely woman a very
important lesson . . .**

THE little brown alarm clock had always worked perfectly. For 10 years it had sat on Miss Brean's bedside table, keeping excellent time, and sprung loudly into life each morning at exactly seven o'clock. Until one morning when — it didn't. And that was the start of Miss Brean's extraordinary day.

Complete
Story
by
**MELODY
RYAN**

117

A LESSON FOR LIVING

When she awoke, she knew that something was wrong. She glanced automatically at the clock — and felt quite stunned with horror. Then she gasped, sprang out of bed and grabbed hold of the clock.

It was half past eight and she should, at that moment, have been sitting down at her desk at Barratt & Brown Ltd., ready to undertake her day's duties as Senior Administrative Officer.

That she should be late — even by five minutes — was unthinkable. Miss Brean had always been proud of the fact that she was one of the most efficient, reliable and highly-respected officers that Barratt & Brown had ever employed. In almost 15 years of working for them, she had never once stepped out of line, never once done anything that was not well thought out and carefully planned.

For a few terrible moments, Miss Brean stood clutching the alarm clock in total confusion. She could not understand why the alarm had not rung; she had no idea how she could have slept on, oblivious to the advancing day. It was quite simply dreadful.

She hurried to the bathroom and proceeded to wash and dress hastily, her mind filled with anxious thoughts. If she went without breakfast and skipped watering the plants, then she should be able to catch the nine o'clock bus. She'd arrive about nine-thirty.

"Good gracious!" Miss Brean paused in the act of pulling back the curtains, and stared in astonishment. There was a man in her garden! A very suspicious-looking character, too, wrapped in a long raincoat, and creeping stealthily among the fruit trees.

MISS BREAN watched, first in amazement, then with mounting indignation. Some sort of tramp or scrounger — after her apples, no doubt. Angrily she marched downstairs and in a moment was striding out of the back door and across the lawn. She squelched briskly over the soggy grass until she reached the intruder.

"And what, may I ask, are you doing in my garden?"

The man, who had been crouched on the grass, peering into the gooseberry bushes, wheeled round at the sound of her voice, almost falling into the mud.

"Oh! Oh — I — er . . . I'm most terribly sorry, Miss Brean." He straightened up to face her, and Miss Brean found herself looking into grey eyes, set deep in a tanned face.

"Oh," she said, somewhat taken aback, "it's you, Mr James."

"I'm terribly sorry, Miss Brean," he repeated, "but I can explain." A trace of defensiveness came into his face, and his eyes hardened.

Miss Brean waited stonily.

She did not like Mr James. Not that she knew a great deal about him, of course — only that he lived in the house next-door-but-one, and appeared to have no family or friends.

"I realise that I am intruding upon your property, Miss Brean. Normally I would have knocked and asked your permission, but I thought that you would be at work."

"I usually am, but today —" She stopped abruptly. Why should she offer him an explanation?

"Well, assuming that you were out," continued Mr James, "I took the liberty of coming into your garden to see if I could find Tashi."

"Tashi?" Miss Brean was feeling confused. This was proving to be a most irregular sort of day.

"My kitten. I've only had him a week, and he's never been outside before." His voice faltered just a little, before he added brusquely, "I was sure you would have no objection, in the circumstances."

Miss Brean softened a little, and the anger faded from her face.

"I see. How long has he been missing?"

"I've searched the house, my garden, my neighbours' gardens, and walked up and down the street, but there's just no sign of him."

"He must have slipped out without me noticing." For a moment he looked so distressed that Miss Brean felt quite sorry for him.

"What does, er, Tashi, look like?" she asked.

"He's ginger, and very tiny." Mr James sighed, then suddenly seemed to pull himself together. "Anyway," he said stiffly, "don't let me waste any more of your time."

"Oh, please feel free to come back and look again, if you wish," Miss Brean said. "I do hope you find him."

Mr James nodded and walked off, and Miss Brean sighed. It really was a shame about the kitten.

She hurried inside, suddenly remembering the urgency of her situation. With a sinking heart, she realised that she had no chance now of catching the nine o'clock bus.

"Oh well." She sighed. "I just hope there is one at nine-thirty." She consulted her bus time-table and found to her relief that there was. It can't be helped, she thought to herself.

At precisely quarter past nine, Miss Brean set off for the bus stop. In her handbag was the alarm clock which would have to be taken to the jeweller's to be mended.

She reached the bus stop at twenty-five past, and stood waiting impatiently.

Suddenly a small movement attracted her attention. She was sure — yes, there it was again. Amid the greenery of the hedge behind her, there was a small ginger blur.

Cautiously, she advanced towards the hedge, bent down, holding her breath — and met the interested stare of a tiny ginger kitten.

At that moment, the bus came rumbling around the corner, and Miss Brean stared at it in dismay. She couldn't miss this bus — cats could find their own way home, she reasoned. But still she could not forget the concern in Mr James's eyes.

And so it came about that Miss Brean found herself on her hands and knees on the wet earth of a stranger's garden, crawling awkwardly through a tangle of shrubbery, and calling in what she hoped was a voice of gentle persuasion.

"Come on, Tashi. There's a good puss. Good puss." She hoped that no-one had seen her creep through the gate in the hedge. And she fervently hoped that there was no-one at home in the house beyond the shrubbery.

"Come along, Tashi — no, no, don't wriggle away. Please!" she whispered.

"What are you doing?" Miss Brean nearly jumped out of her skin. She managed to twist round sufficiently to see a young woman with dark wavy hair, and equally dark eyes which were, at that moment, huge with surprise.

"Oh, er, I am sorry. Look, I know it's strange, and I do know how you feel, believe me, to find a trespasser in your garden, but you see . . ." She brushed a fallen spray of creeper from her eyes.

"But what are you doing?" the girl asked, crouching down in a friendly sort of way, so that she was on a level with Miss Brean.

"Well, you see, I'm trying to catch my, er, my neighbour's kitten; at least, I do hope this *is* his kitten . . .

"Oh, no!" she cried out in alarm. "Look, there he goes!"

The kitten had fled the shrubbery, and was racing joyfully across the lawn towards the house. The young woman, however, had taken command of the situation and sprinted after the kitten, leaving Miss Brean to extricate herself from the shrubbery and follow on behind.

At a most unladylike pace she crossed the lawn and rounded the side of the house, following the young woman. She went through the open back door, and into the kitchen, and was immediately engulfed by the smell of baking. Uncertainly, she paused in the doorway, blinking at a room which seemed full of children.

"Look, Mummy, here — he's under here," she heard one of the children say. "Under the table, Mummy — quick!"

"Pussy, Mummy! 'Ook — Pussy!" This was obviously a younger child.

"Come on, then, Kitty — come here, then." Another child spoke. Embarrassed at the chaos she was causing, Miss Brean hesitated. But the young woman grabbed her arm, pulling her right into the kitchen and shutting the door.

"Right," she said triumphantly, "we've got him!"

"I really am sorry to put you to all this trouble," Miss Brean said, "but I'm sure that my neighbour will be so pleased to have his kitten returned."

The young woman grinned, apparently not at all put out by her very unexpected visit.

"Glad to be of help," she said. "Now then, kids, out of the way. You're frightening the poor little thing."

"Is it your pussycat?" A little girl was staring at Miss Brean with unconcerned curiosity.

"Well, er, no, he —"

"Whose is he, then? What's his name?" The little girl sucked her sticky fingers and added, without waiting for an answer to her question, "We've been helping Mum."

"So I see," Miss Brean said, glancing over the number of mixing bowls, cake tins and wooden spoons that littered the little kitchen. Onions and carrots stood on the table in various states of preparation.

"Do you like cakes?" the child enquired. "I do. And there's bread in the oven. My name's Linda," the little girl continued. "What's your name?"

Miss Brean peered under the table at the kitten, who was quite still, looking bemused.

"My name is Miss Brean."

"Miss Bean," replied the child solemnly. "Bean. Like Baked Bean!" And she dissolved into giggles.

"Now then, Linda," reproved her mother. She turned to Miss Brean. "I think the kitten's worn out with his adventures. Shall we try and entice him out with a saucer of milk?"

"Well, that might be a good idea, if you don't mind?" agreed Miss Brean. "He's probably hungry after all his running around."

"I'll get it, Mum. I'll get some milk." An older child emerged rapidly from under the table and made a dive for the fridge.

"You wait there, Kitty," he instructed, "and see what I've got for you. I —" There was a crash of glass.

"Oh, no, Jimmy!" His mother stared in horror at the smashed bottle amid its sea of milk.

THE flustered Miss Brean hurried to assist in cleaning up the mess, while the toddler wailed louder, and the kitten, unable to bear any more, made a sudden dash across the kitchen. It took a flying leap at the towel rail, embedded its claws in a large yellow towel, and with a plaintive mew, held on for dear life as towel and kitten slithered to a heap on the floor.

When bottle and contents had been cleared up, and the howling child pacified, the young woman turned crossly to Jimmy.

"Why did you have to do that?" She sighed. "That was all the milk we had. What am I going to do?"

Oh dear, thought Miss Brean. Why is everything getting so complicated?

"Please don't tell him off," she ventured, tentatively. "After all, this is all really my fault."

"Oh, no — of course it isn't," the woman said quickly. "I really should have ordered an extra pint today, but the truth is, I thought I had more than that in the fridge. Well, I shall have to get some milk. I'm expecting a friend over for coffee later . . ." She tailed off, looking suddenly hopeful.

"I say, I don't suppose you could keep an eye on the kids while I nip out for more milk. I'll just be ten minutes."

Miss Brean sighed inwardly. Children made her feel uncomfortable and on edge. But she smiled politely, and said that yes, of course it would be all right, and that it was the least she could do.

The young woman beamed. She put on her coat, and searched for her purse.

"Oh — and could you keep an eye on the bread for me? The small loaves can come out of the oven soon, and then the sponges can go in," she added quickly. "Would you mind? Thanks awfully."

With a hasty bang of the door, she was gone.

MISS BREAN eyed her charges warily. Then she rubbed her eyes. It seemed to her that everything was becoming a little unreal — like some ridiculous dream.

"Miss Bean? Can our cakes go in now, Miss Bean?" Linda was licking a dripping spoon as she spoke, and her face was sticky with cake mix.

Miss Brean remembered that she was supposed to check the bread.

"Wait a minute." She went over to the oven and saw that the loaves were, if anything, rather overdone. She put on a pair of old and grubby oven-gloves, and carefully removed the tray.

"All right. Bring the cakes over here," she instructed.

"I'll put them in. I'm older than you, Lucy." Linda snatched the tins from her sister as she spoke, but was met with a wail of protest from the youngster.

"No — no! I want to do it. Let me do it!"

Miss Brean shut the oven door, and hastened to intervene.

"I'll put them in myself," she said. "The oven is very hot, and you might burn yourselves."

The children ignored her, and continued to struggle with the cake tins, in a flurry of long, dark hair and sticky hands.

Miss Brean watched dismayed as both tins landed upside down on the kitchen floor.

The two little girls went down on their hands and knees, trying to scoop up the mixture. But Miss Brean was adamant.

"You'll have to throw it away. The floor is dirty — you can't possibly use the mixture now." The younger child, inevitably, burst into tears, then the toddler began to cry again, which prompted Linda and Jimmy to shout at them both. Miss Brean cringed, and felt totally inadequate.

"I want cakes for my tea." This outcry caused even more noise from the children.

Miss Brean drew a deep breath, picked up a wooden spoon, and, with sudden determination, rapped loudly upon the table.

"Be quiet. All of you." There was an immediate and amazed silence. Four pairs of eyes turned to Miss Brean. Feeling extremely gratified, she relaxed a little and tried to speak calmly.

"Now then, listen. The first thing to do is to get cleared up. Lucy, I want you to collect up all the dirty dishes. Linda, you clear up the mess on the floor. I will do the washing-up and, Jimmy, you can wipe. And perhaps, if you are good, your mother will let you make some more cakes later on."

Their faces brightened a little. "No, she won't," Jimmy said gloomily. "There's no more flour. Lucy upset all what was left; she knocked it on the floor."

"Dear me," Miss Brean said, "you children certainly do seem prone to upsetting things." Then, as Lucy's mouth began to tremble, she added hastily, "Oh, well, never mind. You can make some cakes another day."

"But my friend Annie is coming to tea," Linda said. "And I told her we was having cakes."

"*Were* having cakes," Miss Brean corrected. "Well, it can't be helped, can it?"

Their mother had still not returned, even when all the clearing up was finished.

"What shall we do now?" Linda asked. "Shall I get out my painting things? Then Lucy and me could paint you a picture."

Miss Brean had visions of all the catastrophies that could occur with runny paint and jars of water.

"Oh, I don't think so, dear," she said quickly. "Why don't you all come and sit quietly round the table?"

The children sat down, and looked at Miss Brean expectantly.

"Will you tell us a story, Miss Bean?" Linda asked. "Ooh, yes!" Lucy said eagerly. "Tell us a story."

"Oh dear." Miss Brean sighed. "I don't think I know many stories."

However, she valiantly embarked on the tale of Little Red Riding Hood, and found plenty of willing assistance in her listeners, whenever her memory failed her.

In only a short while Miss Brean began to almost enjoy herself — although she kept an anxious eye on the clock.

A LESSON FOR LIVING

At last the back door opened. The young woman came in, dripping wet, and loaded with shopping.

"Whew! It's raining quite hard now. I'm ever so sorry to have been so long, Miss Brean. The shop was so crowded. Have the kids been good?"

"Yes, very good. We just had one slight accident." She explained about the cake mix.

"Oh, dear — and I didn't think to get any flour." She dumped the bag of shopping down on the floor. "Oh, well — we'll just have to do without cakes."

Linda pouted, and Miss Brean cast her a stern glance. The child blinked and sniffed.

"I'll explain to Annie what happened," the little girl muttered. "She won't mind."

"Good girl," Miss Brean said briskly. She stood up. "And now, I really must be going."

"Oh — won't you stay for a cup of coffee?" asked the young woman. "I have plenty of milk now!"

"Thank you — but no. My neighbour must be very worried about his kitten. I really must return it at once."

"Oh, yes — of course. I'm sorry you had to wait so long. But please do call in and have a coffee some time, won't you?"

"Thank you," Miss Brean said. "That is very kind of you." The young woman smiled.

"By the way, I don't think I told you — my name is Ellie Clarke." She hesitated, then added, "You know, Miss Brean, I've often seen you from my bedroom window when you've been waiting at the bus stop in the mornings. It's been so nice, actually meeting you."

Miss Brean was surprised.

"Well," she said, a bit awkwardly, "it's been nice meeting you. I, er, I don't really know many people around here."

"Well, you will come again, won't you? Just drop in any time."

Keeping a gentle but firm hold on the kitten, Miss Brean took her leave. The children said their goodbyes, and stood waving at the kitchen door.

" 'Bye, Pussy. 'Bye, Miss Bean. 'Bye."

At least the rain had stopped, Miss Brean thought as she marched up the street. In fact, it even looked as if the sun was trying to break through, for a patch of yellow glowed dully behind a grey cloud.

Miss Brean considered the events of the morning as she strode along. It was all quite incredible, really. And she hadn't phoned the office. She would do that after she had returned the kitten and simply explain she'd been unavoidably delayed, but that she was on her way. That would have to satisfy them.

Mr James had a green front gate. Miss Brean pushed it open, walked up the straight path, with its neat border of rose bushes, and rang the doorbell.

"Why, Miss Brean . . ."

"Good morning, again, Mr James. I think — at least I hope — that this is your kitten?"

Mr James stared at her. An expression of disbelief crossed his face, then melted into pure joy.

"Yes — oh, yes! That's my Tashi! But how — where —?"

"It's rather a long story, Mr James, but I am also very glad to be able to return him to you."

"I can't believe it — really it's . . . but do please come in, Miss Brean."

She stepped into the narrow hall. "I'm afraid I can only stay a moment."

Mr James cradled the cat in his arms.

"I really am so grateful — I don't know how to thank you." He looked wonderingly at Miss Brean, intrigued by the slightly-dishevelled picture she presented. Despite her untidy appearance he noticed she was smiling and her cheeks were softly pink.

"Well, I really must go now, Mr James," Miss Brean said. "I hope that Tashi will be none the worse for his adventure."

"I'm sure that he'll be fine. You know," Mr James stroked the soft bundle in his arms, "I really was afraid that I had lost him for good. I haven't had him for long but already he means so much to me. Life is not so, er, lonely, if you know what I mean."

"Yes, I understand what you mean." For a moment, a look of sadness passed over Miss Brean's face, then she said softly, "Well, goodbye, Mr James."

"Goodbye, Miss — no, wait." A sudden idea had come to him. He cleared his throat.

"I just wondered if — I mean don't feel obliged to, or anything — I just wondered if you would care to come and have tea with me this afternoon. It would be my way of saying thank you, for all your trouble."

Miss Brean was taken aback. She hesitated for a moment, then made up her mind.

"Thank you. I — I think I'd like that. Very much."

"Oh! Oh — you would? Well, er, come about five then, if that's all right? I'm on holiday this week."

How strange, Miss Brean thought, as she hurried across the road to the telephone kiosk. I have always thought him such a dis-agreeable man. But perhaps, maybe after all, he was just shy and rather lonely.

Whoever would have thought he would have invited me to tea? But then — she smiled to herself as she picked up the receiver and began to dial — whoever would have thought that I would have accepted?

BARRATT & BROWN were relieved to hear from Miss Brean. They had feared she was ill, or that she had been involved in an accident. Miss Brean explained, then, with a polite apology for the inconvenience caused, she said she would be taking the whole day off, as part of her annual holiday entitlement.

For a moment there was a stunned silence. Could this really be Miss Brean speaking?

"I shall, of course, be returning to work tomorrow. Now, if you will excuse me, I have a great deal to do."

"Yes, well, er, Miss Brean . . . we'll see you tomorrow, then."

Miss Brean strode back across the street to her house. She felt a sweet, warm sense of release seeping through her, and a delicious tingle of accomplishment. She was glowing quietly as she brushed the mud from her coat, placed it upon a hanger, and began to busy herself in the kitchen.

Good, there was a tin of cocoa in the larder — that meant she could make chocolate cakes; little tiny chocolate cakes, with pink and white icing. The children would be delighted when she took them round — and perhaps Ellie would invite her to stay for a cup of tea.

Of course, she would be sure to be home before five o'clock, to change into her best blue dress, ready for tea with Mr James.

She began to hum softly as she got out her large china mixing bowl. For Mr James she would make a big sponge — and perhaps one or two little cakes as well. That would be a nice surprise for him.

Suddenly, Miss Brean jumped and gasped, for the peace of the little kitchen had been shattered by a shrill burst of sound: an explosion of ringing. For a moment she was mystified — and then realised that the source of the noise was inside her handbag. Miss Brean began to smile, then to laugh.

She picked up the bag, and took out her alarm clock.

"You!" she exclaimed, wiping her eyes, and laughing still more.

"I had forgotten all about you. You were the cause of everything — do you know that?"

As the clock stopped ringing, she told herself that she really must remember to get it fixed tomorrow. Perhaps, in fact, the jeweller's would advise her to throw it away. Not that she would, of course. She'd probably buy a new one but she would never part with the old clock. She had just discovered that she was quite attached to it. □

PASSING STRANGERS

They walked along the
    country road,
  He walking up, she
  walking down,
She with a collie on a
    leash
  He with an aged, sluggish
  hound.

Too shy to pass the time
    of day
  They gave a smile or a nod
  of head,
Then he went up and she
    went down,
  One being pulled, the
  other led.

And so it was they came to
    meet
  Quite often on this daily
  walk,
The canines greeting like
    old chums,
  The humans who had yet
  to talk.

Until one day they both
    exchanged
  The names of their four-
  legged friends,
He turned around, they
  both walked down
  The road to where this
  story ends.

        — C. H., Treorchy.

Complete
Story by
ISOBEL
STEWART

TWO

DIFFERENT WORLDS

In his modern, efficient, stream-lined world, what place was there for an old-fashioned thing like love?

BETH was an old-fashioned girl — she believed in old-fashioned things like politeness, cups of tea, log fires in winter, family holidays, living at home, love at first sight and marriage.

Most of all, she believed in love at first sight. So she wasn't in the least surprised when she fell in love with Martin Kennedy the moment she met him.

All right, he wasn't quite the sort of man she had imagined herself falling in love with. Her earlier imaginings had been of a tall, fair-haired man — a poet, or at the very least a man who enjoyed reading poetry.

Martin Kennedy wasn't in the least like that. He was tall, certainly, but he was dark-haired, and with the most determined jaw Beth had ever seen. He came to the small firm Beth worked for to re-organise their time and efficiency.

There was no doubt at all that he would make a good job of it. He carried a small notebook around with him, he observed everyone as they worked, and then made notes.

TWO DIFFERENT WORLDS

When she had known him for two days, Beth came to the regretful conclusion that Martin had probably never, by choice, opened a poetry book in his life. And if he should ever now decide to read Shakespeare, he would probably work out a way in which the bard could have written Hamlet in half the time.

But, of course, it didn't matter by then. She could pinpoint it to the moment he had stood looking down at her, shaken her hand firmly and politely, and had told her that he was going to have her desk moved. That way she would waste less time walking along the corridor to take dictation from old Mr Jones.

"I don't mind walking," Beth told him truthfully and shyly.

"It wastes time," Martin told her severely. And then he smiled, a warm smile that turned Beth's already unsteady heart right over.

It was as simple as that. Beth was lost. She would have followed him anywhere in the world, carrying his little black notebook for him.

If she got the chance.

But before long she began to realise that Martin was much too modern, efficient and streamlined to believe in love at first sight. He would probably, Beth thought sadly, want to make up a list in his little black notebook of the points for and against two people falling in love.

AND so she was very surprised indeed when Martin stopped at her desk, on the last day of his assignment, and coughed.

She took off her glasses and looked up at him, blinking a little because she was very short-sighted, and as soon as her glasses were off, everyone became a little hazy.

"I wondered," Martin said carefully, "if you would have dinner with me tomorrow night."

Beth couldn't believe it. She thought he had hardly noticed her, once he had had her desk moved.

"Tomorrow night?" she repeated, still wondering if this was really happening.

"I'll be finished here by then, you see," Martin explained. "On principle, you know, I keep business and pleasure apart. I'm sure you understand."

She certainly could understand that. It was the sort of old-fashioned principle she lived by herself.

"Thank you, I would like that," she replied softly.

When she got home that night, she told her mother and her father and her young sister Emily about her date with Martin.

"I'll do your face for you," her sister offered generously.

Beth thanked her, a little doubtfully.

"Why don't you pin your hair up?" her mother suggested. "It makes you look more — well, more the kind of girl this Martin is probably used to."

Her father, from behind his newspaper, muttered that she was fine just as she was. However, Beth decided that maybe Mother knew best.

It's win or lose, she told herself, the following evening as she walked towards Martin. With Emily's help she had her hair up into a sophisticated style and she'd made her face up carefully.

It was lose.

From the first moment, the dinner date was a disaster.

BETH could see that far from being impressed by her new look, Martin was somewhat taken aback. And once she realised this, she could do nothing but retreat into herself, so that by the end of the meal her throat was so tight with disappointment that it was all she could do to murmur a reply to anything he said.

At last, in desperation she thought, he talked about the office, and the changes that had been made.

"I'm sure you find you get through much more work, now that your desk is in the little room beside Mr Jones?" he asked.

"Well, yes and no," Beth said carefully, glad to be on neutral ground now. "You see, while I don't have to walk backwards and forwards for dictation, I have to walk the other way to go and make tea for Mr Jones when he wants it."

"Tea?" Martin repeated, surprised. "But you shouldn't be making tea — there's the canteen service now that brings tea at eleven and three-thirty."

"Yes, but Mr Jones often wants a cup of tea when it isn't the right time," she explained.

Martin sighed.

And with that sigh, Beth accepted defeat.

Perhaps she had fallen in love with him at first sight, but they were far too different, she and Martin. She should have seen from the start that nothing could possibly come of this. Quite suddenly, all she wanted was for the disastrous evening to finish.

They left the restaurant, and he helped her into his car and drove her home, talking politely. He was surprised that she lived at home with her family and she told him she preferred it that way. He was even more surprised at the distance out in the country she lived. Beth, too disappointed to tell him about her mother's hens, the beloved old horse, and George the St Bernard, just said that yes, it was quite a distance.

Martin drew up outside the house, and Beth thanked him politely and untruthfully for a pleasant evening. He said that he would ring her, and she thanked him. But they both knew that he wouldn't.

And that was it.

Beth went inside, and Martin drove away.

Carefully, conscientiously, she creamed all the make-up off her face, and washed it, and then she unpinned her hair and got into her nightie and her comfortable old blue dressing-gown.

Then she made herself a cup of tea, and sat down at the embers of the fire and cried into George's shaggy but comforting coat.

Then George suddenly stood up, almost making her lose her balance, and she realised that there was a soft but insistent knocking at the front door.

Martin stood there. His dark hair was untidy, and there was a smear of dirt down one cheek.

"I ran out of petrol," he said. "I wondered if your father had a spare can in the garage."

"We can look and see," Beth replied, surprised at how breathless she felt. "But I shouldn't think so."

She was right, there was no spare petrol. A little helplessly, she looked at the now somewhat untidy business efficiency expert.

"We could siphon some out of Dad's car," she suggested. "I know he has a pump somewhere because Mum often runs out of petrol."

A little hampered by George's desire to make friends with this unexpected visitor, they eventually found the pump, and Martin siphoned enough petrol into a can that Beth had found, to get him back to town.

"Please apologise to your father from me," Martin said stiffly. "I'll return the can and the petrol as soon as possible."

Beth took him into the kitchen to wash his hands, and it was only as she handed him the kitchen towel, and he looked down at her, that she realised completely just how she looked. And there was something in Martin's dark eyes — amusement, and something else — that told her he was well aware of this, too.

Defensively, she said, "And how come someone as efficient as you ran out of petrol?"

He coloured.

"I forgot," he admitted, "because I was — kind of agitated about taking you out."

This admission left Beth completely speechless, and she could do nothing but look at him in stunned silence.

"I'd better go," Martin said then. "My car's about two miles down the road."

And all at once, on top of everything else, the thought of the efficient Martin Kennedy trudging down a country lane at midnight, carrying a can of petrol, was too much for her. She began to laugh.

After a moment Martin began to laugh too. George the St Bernard liked to see people laughing, and he wagged his tail in appreciation.

Then, somehow or other, and Beth was never quite sure how, she and Martin weren't laughing any longer, they were looking at each other, and it seemed to Beth that the whole world was standing still, waiting.

Then Martin kissed her.

IT was a long, long time before he let her go. So long that George had settled down on the floor at their feet, and gone to sleep.

"Beth," Martin murmured, unsteadily. "Oh, Beth, love."

And he kissed her again.

"You know what I'd like, more than anything?" he murmured, much later, as his lips reluctantly left hers.

Beth couldn't imagine.

"I'd like a cup of tea," Martin said wistfully. "Would your parents think it dreadful if I have a cup of tea with you in the kitchen in the middle of the night, before I've even met them, and before I've had the chance to ask your father if I can marry his daughter?"

While Beth was still recovering from this, George woke up and rolled over on to his back, his huge paws waving in the air. Absently, Martin tickled George's tummy with one foot. And it was then that Beth knew that everything was going to be absolutely, wonderfully right.

After all, what objections could her parents possibly have to a man who knew when George wanted his tummy tickled and who admitted to needing a cup of tea.

"How do you like your tea?" she asked.

"Strong," Martin told her positively.

He watched her for a little while.

"Beth, love," he said after a moment, "surely you'd be better to carry the kettle over to the sink? You've made three journeys across the kitchen instead of two, with that jug in your hand. Now if you think about it — "

Beth looked at him, and with complete clarity she saw a future stretching ahead of her, with Martin telling her the most efficient way to clean the house, change nappies, make feeds, organise school lifts, pack for holidays. And she knew that because it was Martin, she wouldn't mind at all.

But at the same time —

"Martin," she said softly, firmly, "when I make tea, I'll do it my way. When you make tea, you can do it your way. All right?"

And just to make sure he took her point in the right spirit, she stood on tiptoe and this time she kissed him. □

The Guardian

THE farm was better guarded than anyone knew, but it took some time to realise this.

The ducks were the main problem: no-one knew why they had chosen to come to this farm, but come they had. Once they settled, it became necessary to guard them against the foxes. Although they were wild birds, they decided to live as farm birds.

There were four of them, handsome birds, with their green heads and bright orange bands around their bodies. Each year, on the beaches where they'd lived before, they had lost their babies to fierce dogs. So they had come here, where the dogs knew better than to touch the ducklings, and where people fed them. It was a far easier life.

Baby had named them. She was two, but no-one ever called her anything but Baby, as her real name, Geraldine, didn't seem to

The stallion was king of the farmyard, and he knew exactly how to defend his little kingdom.

suit her. She was an energetic, noisy little girl, often in the way. She was just too fearless for her own good.

She herded the ducks and two big Alsatians, and the cross-bred collie which the dustmen had found, scavenging, and brought to the farm. She herded the cats, she herded the three mares and the stallion.

She would stand in the field and call to the horses, and Majesty reared and waved his forehooves at her, and she laughed. The mares cantered off, their manes and tails waving in the wind, and Baby laughed. People called her to come in and to come away, but she still laughed.

GELDART

Complete Story by JOYCE STRANGER

THE GUARDIAN

THE biggest duck was Puddle Duck, because she preferred the muddy puddles to the ciean farm pool. Baby always rushed after her, making sure she was in by dusk. She loved Puddle Duck more than the others, and was delighted when an uncle found a book about Jemima Puddleduck and gave it to her for Christmas.

The second duck was Quarrel Duck, as aggressive as any farm wife. She was forever rushing after the other three, apparently berating them — she made more noise than all the others put together. Sometimes, Baby could be heard yelling at her to shut up.

The third duck was Muddle Duck, who never quite knew where the others were. If they were in the big field, she was in the little one, frantically calling to them. If they were in the little field, she would be searching the reeds at the edge of the pond in the big field, yelling to them to wait, she was coming.

The last was Pretty Duck. This was the drake. He had his own ideas about a duck's life and most of his was spent in the stallion's stable, where interesting bits of food were dropped and he could eat twice as much as his wives.

It was the cross-bred collie who herded the ducks most enthusiastically. He was fed on duck eggs and soon discovered that they only appeared in the straw, and that they only appeared when the ducks were there.

So he spent a lot of his time satisfying his herding instincts by driving the ducks into their box, which was very useful at night, but remarkably annoying during the day. This was because the ducks objected by setting up such a noise that everything else in the farmyard yelled, too.

But the collie-cross was sure that once they were safely in, there would be more eggs. And he adored ducks' eggs, hard boiled and cut up in his evening feed.

So between the dog and Baby, the ducks led quite a busy life. But they led an even busier one when the mares and the stallion were out, as the mares were very curious about these creatures that came to the pool and swam there, unafraid of anything.

Susie, the Shetland pony, would stand in the water and try to encourage them out on to the land, sure that water was bad for ducks. Queen, the big old mare who had long been retired from breeding, took an even more active interest, perhaps missing her foals and wishing she could mother these creatures.

She was even more interested when Quarrel Duck managed to foil the collie-cross by hiding the eggs and hatching out seven fluffy ducklings. Ducklings, Queen was sure, should not swim and she haunted the pond edge, trying to keep them away.

Numa, who was in foal, had no time for the ducks.

It would be her third foal, and she adored her babies, driving herself mad by her relentless need to keep them safe.

She chased endlessly after each foal, keeping it away from the other mares, or the fence.

Majesty ignored the ducks. He was far too proud for such creatures.

There was one other animal that was enormously interested in the ducks. That was the fox who hunted in the coppice. Night after night he stalked the farm, his mouth watering as he smelled duck, but their box was foxproof and he could not break in, so he took to lying in the bushes, watching.

One day he might find one of them alone and make a quick sortie, and duck certainly tasted good.

The adults on the farm were always busy.

There were the horses to muck out when they were stabled at night, the yard to hose down, the feed to give. The animals all needed grooming, they needed the attentions of the blacksmith and sometimes of the vet, and there were the goats and the cows to be milked.

There were the hens to clean out and the eggs to collect and the geese to watch against, as they had a habit of suddenly flying at anyone who wasn't looking.

Baby always stood her ground and yelled at them, but the others weren't as confident.

ALL that summer, the fox was aware of the busy life of the farm and of Baby in particular. Nobody could ever ignore her. It was a wonder, her mother would say irritably, that she didn't end up in the pond with the ducks, drowned.

It was a wonder, her father would say, that she didn't end up in the baler or the milk churn, or under the tractor.

She moved like quicksilver, and was always racing from place to place. The man who looked after the horses wondered that she wasn't trampled, the way she stood among them when they were racing around the field.

Majesty often looked as if he were within an ace of rushing right over her, but somehow, even in his maddest moments, he never did.

THE GUARDIAN

Majesty was aware of the fox and of fox smell and he didn't like it. He stood at the fence, his sensitive ears moving forwards and backwards, his large eyes trying to make out what creature lay in the bushes. Sometimes he called to the mares.

Numa, the least curious and the most preoccupied, never answered. Queen came and stood beside him, trying to see what he was seeing, but her sense of smell wasn't strong enough for her to know it was fox. Susie, aware of the sharp and musky tang, reared and pranced, and those on the farm wondered what had set her off.

Baby, living in her own world, continued to herd the ducks and to try to drive the horses home at night. She continued to command the dogs, sending them to their beds, or to the barn, or telling them they were bad so that they remained in a continuous state of confusion. She was totally unpredictable and also, usually, wrong.

"*Bad* Spot," she would yell at the collie-cross, asleep in the sun, so that he woke up and tried desperately to work out what he was doing wrong and tried to find another place where he wouldn't be bad. But Baby would follow him and tell him off, so that in the end he took to creeping behind the stallion's manger, in the darkness where she never thought of looking for him.

One sunny summer day, the horses were out in the big field, and the ducks were on the pond. The family had gone out, except for the man who looked after the horses.

He had groomed the stallion and put him out to graze, and now he was sitting in the sunlight on the edge of the little stone wall, thinking of nothing in particular, when he heard a commotion in the field. He turned to look.

He was too far away to do anything about it. He could only shout. But the wind was strong, and his words were blown away.

Quarrel Duck had come out of the pond on the side away from the horses, and had begun to make her way steadily round the verge. The fox saw his chance. He raced across, and sprang, and Quarrel Duck was caught in his strong jaws. The noise she made drowned every other noise on the farm.

Majesty turned his head.

The fox was speeding towards the wood, making for the fence, which he could scale like a cat. Quarrel Duck, obviously far from dead, was screaming at the top of her very considerable voice, while the other three ducks added their moans and wails to the din.

The fox was several hundred yards from the stallion and racing as fast as he could, but Quarrel Duck was large and heavy, and a remarkably awkward mouthful.

Majesty reared, and roared, making a sound that the man had never heard before from any horse's throat.

It was a long way to the fox for Majesty, but the water was shallow. The stallion splashed through, sending up fountains of sparkling drops and splatters of mud. The fox heard the thunder of hooves behind him and raced on. He was tiring. The duck had definitely been a mistake, and her struggles as she flapped and tried to bat at his face with her beak were beginning to exhaust him.

The speeding hooves came nearer.

The watching man stared.

Majesty reached the fox and turned his back. His powerful hind legs struck the fox in the ribs and sent him rolling. He dropped Quarrel Duck, who dashed off at high speed in an ungainly flying waddle, quacking at the top of her voice. Majesty turned and sped towards the fox, and his hooves struck again and again.

The fox crept away to heal his wounds, and to remember for the rest of his life that it was unwise to hunt on this farm.

MAJESTY followed Quarrel Duck back to the gate, where the other ducks joined her, and Majesty nosed them along the ground, pushing them relentlessly towards the man, and safety.

Majesty stood and waited, watching. The man came forward and lifted Quarrel Duck, discovering that the odd walk had been caused by two broken legs. She was also covered in bites. He took her and splinted the legs and injected antibiotic. That night, she went to the vet, who treated her with wound dressing.

From that day on, the ducks had an extra herder, as the stallion would never let them reach that field again. He checked them and guarded them, and pushed them back towards their box. The drake found his own way of getting to water, but all the ducks had to content themselves with the muddy puddles, so Baby had to name them all Puddle Ducks.

Quarrel Duck was unable at first to follow them. In the long weeks during which her wounds healed, she spent her time in Majesty's stable, and at night refused to be herded back to her own bed. She slept in the manger, and in the mornings the collie-cross discovered that there would always be an egg there.

But he knew it wasn't his, and left it there, as a gift to the stallion that had saved Quarrel Duck's life.

People passing often look in wonder at the stallion in the yard. Always, in front of him, there's a big duck. Whenever he stops to rest, she folds herself neatly at his hooves and looks up at him, admiration in her eyes.

And she will have nothing at all to do with the drake, now. □

Teacher's

**What was she doing, thinking
of herself in that way?
It was her son who was
his pupil!**

RESCUING Gary's lunch-box from under his bed on Saturday morning, Janet found the note. She smoothed it out, and read what it said:

For those parents who have expressed interest, there will be a special evening class in mathematics, once a week, on Tuesday evenings at eight. Mr Taylor, our senior mathematics master, has agreed to take these classes.

Pet

**Complete
Story
by
ISOBEL
STEWART**

TEACHER'S PET

Janet went out to find her son. She confronted Gary with the note.

"Oh, did you find it?" he asked, unsurprised. "Sorry, Mum, can't take it. My hands are covered with oil."

"Why didn't you give it to me?" Janet asked. "It's dated three days ago."

"I forgot," Gary replied, and, as always, his lack of deviousness disconcerted her. "But anyway, I didn't think you'd be interested. Maths isn't your scene at all."

"No, I know that," Janet agreed. "But — maybe it's something I should do, so that I can help you with your maths."

"Help with my maths?" her son repeated, and polite as he usually was, he was unable to hide the surprise in his voice. "Oh, Mum, how could you help me with my maths, when you can't even get your bank statements sorted out?"

Janet sat down on the wall beside him.

"Maybe I could help you if I did go to these classes," she suggested. And in spite of her realisation that this was serious, her lips twitched. "And maybe I could keep my bank balance right, too."

Gary straightened up.

"Look, Mum," he said, patiently. "I've told you before, I don't need any help with my maths."

"But what about your marks last term? You only just passed."

"I know," Gary admitted. "But it's like old Tinker said. I could do much better if I worked."

"Tinker?" Janet asked.

"Tinker Taylor," Gary explained. "Mum, Sandra's bike needs a new tube. I'll go down and get one and fix her bike up later today. OK?"

"OK," Janet said absently. "I'll take her for her ballet lessons in the car."

SHE went inside to tell her daughter, and found Sandra earnestly practising at the practice barre Gary had put up for her in her bedroom.

"I'll take you in the car, Sandra," Janet said. "Gary is still mending your bike."

"Good. I can have ten minutes more to practise," Sandra replied, between movements.

And I can have ten minutes for a cup of coffee before I go, Janet thought.

. In the kitchen, she sat down at the table with her mug of coffee and the morning paper. And once again, the vague feeling of guilt was there..

Paul had always hated sitting down at the kitchen table even to drink coffee and having a meal there was almost unforgiveable.

But now, Janet thought half-amused, half-concerned, there's no Paul to dictate where we eat. No doubt he has all his meals properly served in the beautiful dining-room Sandra told me about. With Helen always perfectly dressed, and never without make-up.

It was three years since she and Paul had parted, and even then, at the start, she had known with the same devastating honesty as Gary that she wasn't heartbroken.

They hadn't been happy, really happy, for a long time. And the relief of being herself, instead of trying to be the sort of wife Paul wanted, was wonderful.

There was no doubt the children were happier, too. After the first tears from Sandra, and tight-lipped shock from Gary, the children had settled amazingly well to being a one-parent family, and she had accepted almost total responsibility for them. Which brought her back to maths.

JANET set her coffee cup down. She would go along to the special evening classes, and learn enough to be able to talk to Gary about his maths, maybe discuss his problems with him.

And then, when Sandra, too, ran into problems — which she would do — she would be able to help her, too.

"Mum, you're not!" Gary said obviously appalled, when she told him on Tuesday evening that she was going off to the special maths class at school.

"Yes, I am," Janet replied firmly. "Now, I've got a notebook and pencil — do you think I'll need anything else?"

"What about logarithm tables?" Gary suggested gloomily. And then he obviously decided to try again.

"Look, Mum, you'll be out of your depth. There've been so many changes in maths since your time, and you never did know too much about it, did you?"

"Enough to cope with a few evening classes to bring me up to date," Janet told him, with dignity. "Now, no TV until your homework is finished. And that goes for Sandra."

"You'd better tell her, she won't listen to me," Gary reminded her. He sighed. "You won't have to sign your name on a register or anything, will you?"

"You mean you don't want Mr Taylor to know I'm your mother?" Janet asked him. "You mean you're ashamed of me?"

His grey eyes looked back steadily.

"No, not ashamed," he said honestly. "But embarrassed because you can't count, and you won't understand a word Mr Taylor is saying."

"Nonsense," Janet replied, proud of the crispness of her tone. "Of course I'll understand."

Half an hour later, sitting in the classroom, she looked at what

TEACHER'S PET

Mr Taylor — Jeff Taylor — had written on the blackboard.

Binary relations are the regulations expressing the association between two objects.

"I think we'd better get to grips with this whole binary system first of all," Mr Taylor said brightly.

Mr Taylor, Janet thought, was much younger than she would have expected. About her own age probably, and surprisingly, an outdoors type — he didn't get that tan from sitting inside poring over Pythagoras.

She looked around. There weren't too many people taking advantage of these evening classes, and most of them were men. There were one or two mothers, and they looked bright and alert, making notes from time to time. Janet tried to, but there wasn't enough that she could grasp.

"Right. Any questions?" Mr Taylor asked, looking at his class with an expectant expression.

One of the fathers near the front asked a question, and it took a good ten minutes for Mr Taylor to answer, with a few diagrams on the board, a reference or two to the maths book issued by the school and a mathematical joke.

She understood neither the question, the answer, the diagram, nor the joke. But she smiled dutifully with the rest of the class.

"I think that will do for tonight," Mr Taylor said. He looked around, and Janet was certain that his clear blue eyes fixed on her. "I hope I've made everything clear?"

There were murmurs of assent and appreciation all round. Janet tried to look as alert and responsive as the rest of the class, and at the same time not too eager, as she gathered up her notebook and her pencil, and pulled her short jacket on.

"How did it go?" Gary asked, when she got home.

"Fine — just fine," Janet told him heartily.

"Well, maybe it was a little confusing tonight," she admitted. "But I'm sure by next week I'll see it all much more clearly."

The following Tuesday she thought maybe she was getting a cold. There was this tickle in her throat, she explained to Gary when he came home from school.

"Maybe you won't be able to go to your maths class tonight?" Gary suggested, hopefully.

The same thought had occurred to Janet, but she knew she had to try again.

She laughed. "Let a little thing like a cold keep me away from my maths class, just when I'm beginning to understand what's going on?" she said. "No, I'll take a lemon drink, and I'll be fine."

It must have been the lemon drink, with aspirin in it, that made her head a little muzzy, she thought in the evening. That was why she was having such difficulty following what Mr Taylor was explaining. It must be clear. You could see that from the nods and the appreciative murmurs all around.

She shook her head to clear it, and looked at the board again.

She read the problem on it over and over again. Individually, the words made sense. Put together, they meant nothing.

MR TAYLOR was speaking again, and the class was listening attentively.

Janet listened, too, but now her attention was distracted by a sneeze that was determined not to be stifled, no matter how hard she tried.

It was one of those sneezes that almost lifted the roof off. Mr Taylor stopped what he was saying and waited until the echoes of the sneeze subsided.

"Bless you," he said, pleasantly. "Now as I was saying . . ."

Little of what he was saying meant anything to Janet, who was concentrating on stifling another sneeze.

It must have been the oncoming cold that made her so slow at the end of the class, she thought. For she was still putting her notebook into her shoulderbag when Mr Taylor passed her desk, ready to close the classroom.

"I hope you're all right," he said, smiling. "That sounds like quite a cold you have."

Janet felt her cheeks grow warm.

"It was certainly quite a sneeze," she agreed, slinging her bag over her shoulder.

Mr Taylor looked down at her.

"Are you enjoying the class?" he asked unexpectedly.

"It's — most interesting and stimulating," Janet said quickly. "I'm sure everyone is enjoying it."

They were walking along the corridor now.

"I don't know that I'm too happy about talking to adults in the class situation," Mr Taylor admitted. "But the headmaster said there had been such demand from parents who felt they just needed some help to get to grips with the changes in maths." He smiled.

"So I agreed, with some reservations. I must say I thought it would be mostly fathers who would come along, but I suppose you mathematically-inclined women wouldn't be very impressed by me saying that!"

Janet found she was having difficulty meeting his eyes, and she was glad they had reached the main door.

K

"Whose mother are you?" Mr Taylor asked, interestedly.

"Gary's," Janet told him. "Gary Wood." She hesitated, and then, a little awkwardly, said: "His father and I are divorced, and — I thought I should come along, and — be able to give Gary a hand when he needs it."

Afterwards, she wasn't too sure whether it was doubt or appreciation she saw in Mr Taylor's eyes, as he said goodnight to her.

"How was it tonight?" Gary asked when she got home.

Janet sneezed.

"Well, I wasn't at my best with this cold," she said with perfect truth, "but it was most interesting."

She stopped, trying to remember. "We were talking about functions, and — associations."

"Were you?" Gary asked, with surprise and, she hoped, with respect.

SURPRISINGLY her cold didn't develop, and by the weekend there was no sign of it at all. On Sunday morning Janet woke early, and when she opened her curtains she saw, with delight, that the day had a newly-washed shine about it, and there was a promise of good weather.

We'll have a picnic, she decided, and she dressed quickly and woke Gary and Sandra.

"At the beach?" Sandra asked sleepily.

"Can we take Timmy?" Gary asked, appearing at the door, his hair tousled.

At the sound of his name, the spaniel looked hopefully from one to the other.

"Yes — beach and Timmy," Janet promised. "Hurry up and dress and we'll pack a few sandwiches and go."

They had had lots of picnics during these three years and they worked well as a team to get ready.

Paul had never liked picnics and so, after a few attempts, he hadn't gone on any. He didn't mind going for a drive, stopping off for tea and sandwiches somewhere, but he couldn't, he had told her, get wildly enthusiastic about sitting on the beach with sand in everything, especially the sandwiches.

They walked for miles, with Timmy running ahead, his golden ears flying, his feathered paws making the sand fly, and they ate everything, right down to the last crumb of the last sandwich.

"Old Tinker asked how your cold was, Mum," Gary said casually. He traced a pattern in the sand. "He asked if you were enjoying his classes."

Janet put the flask back into the picnic basket and turned to look at her son.

"What did you tell him?" she asked.

"I said I didn't think you were, much," Gary told her, as honest as ever. "That's true, isn't it?"

In spite of herself, Janet felt a smile tugging at her lips.

"I suppose so," she admitted. "But — I'd rather you hadn't told — er — Mr Taylor. I mean — he must just feel he's wasting his time."

"Oh, he doesn't feel that," Gary assured her. "Actually he's surprised at how much some of the people in the class are enjoying it, he says."

Janet shaded her eyes and looked at Sandra, near the water's edge, moving slowly, trying to get as near as she could to the seagulls on the rocks.

"Is Mr Taylor married?" she asked, her voice as casual as her son's had been.

Gary shook his head.

"I'm surprised," Janet said, thinking of Jeff Taylor, tall, lean and brown, his eyes very blue.

"He's got plenty to do without being married," Gary told her. "He goes sailing, and he climbs and he goes on walking holidays." He shrugged. "Maybe when he's older, and can't do all these things, he'll get married."

"Maybe," Janet agreed, turning away so that he wouldn't see her lips twitching. But along with the amusement there was a deeper feeling which she couldn't quite grasp.

THE following Tuesday, when Janet parked and made her way along the corridor, with its indefinable smell of school, she found that she was walking more and more slowly, although she knew that already she was late.

Janet's heart sank deeper and deeper down at the depressing thought of another hour sitting trying to look as if she understood all those domains and functions and associations.

And then, suddenly, when she turned the corner two classrooms from the maths room, she knew she wasn't going to the class. I'll go right back home, she thought with growing delight, make myself a cup of coffee, and sit with my feet up and read!

Without giving herself time to change her mind, she whirled round, back round the corner of the corridor — and right into the arms of Jeff Taylor, who was hurrying towards his maths class.

"Oh — I'm so sorry." Janet gasped, her cheeks scarlet. "Let me help you pick up your books."

All his books and notes were scattered on the floor, under the impetus of her impulsive turn. She gathered them together, and handed them to him.

"Thanks," Jeff Taylor said. He smiled down at her. "Now what do you do," he asked her, thoughtfully, "with a pupil who is all too clearly going to play hookey?"

Janet hadn't thought her cheeks could become any more scarlet, but they did.

"I wasn't — I mean I just — I forgot —" she began.

TEACHER'S PET

"Give it one more try," Jeff Taylor suggested. "See if you're making any sense out of it tonight, and — let's have a cup of coffee afterwards, and you can tell me what you've decided."

It seemed ungracious to refuse, after practically knocking him down and making him even later for his class, so Janet agreed, a little doubtfully, to give it one more try.

TEN minutes later she knew that her doubts had been justified. More than justified, she thought, reading the latest problem that Jeff Taylor had just written on the board.

She hadn't a clue how to find the answer, and — what's more, she really didn't care.

"You don't need to tell me," Jeff Taylor said to her when the class had finished. "I saw your face when we dealt with the calculus problem, and I knew exactly what you were thinking. You couldn't care less, could you?"

He smiled.

"Like your son, you have a very honest face. Now there's a little place round the corner that makes good coffee. Let's walk round there, and we'll come back for our cars afterwards."

"You don't have to —" she began awkwardly.

"I know," he agreed. "But I want to. I want to know what brought you, with absolutely no interest in maths, to my special class!"

Somehow it wasn't difficult to tell him.

"It's all up to me, you see," she said slowly, feeling for the right words. "I — I wasn't the right sort of wife for Paul. I know that. And I must be the right sort of mother for Gary and Sandra." She tried to smile. "Paul has another wife now, and she's right for him — but the children are stuck with me, so I have to cope. And — that's why I came to your maths class."

There was concern and kindness in Jeff Taylor's blue eyes, and it was so long since anyone had looked at her like that, that all at once her throat was tight.

"Listen to me, Janet," he said, and his voice was firm. "Yes, I asked Gary what your name was, because — well, because I couldn't go on thinking of you as Gary's mother, or even as Mrs Wood.

"Janet — you don't have to be able to help Gary with his maths to be a good mother. In fact, Gary doesn't need help, he just has to get down to working. And I think he's beginning to. But — all right, you're not good at maths. Gary told me that himself. But at the same time, he told me other things that you're good at."

Janet waited, looking at this man who was suddenly no longer a stranger.

"He told me," Jeff Taylor said quietly, "that you're good at all sorts of things. Like making cakes, and like letting Gary and Sandra help you to cook, and not minding the mess. Like listening to them when they tell you things, and taking them on picnics. Like laughing at the jokes they tell you, or crying with them when the old cat died last year."

She looked at him with wonder.

"Gary told you all that about me?" she asked him.

He nodded. "And more," he said simply.

"So you see, Janet — you're doing fine with your kids, and you don't need to feel that you have to do something that isn't exactly right for you."

Like I was always having to do with Paul, Janet thought. But I don't have to now, with Gary and Sandra. I can — I can just be myself.

Jeff Taylor's blue eyes were on her face, and a swift, disturbing certainty came to her. With this man, too, she could be herself. There wouldn't ever be any need to try to be something she wasn't, or to pretend.

She smiled, hesitantly.

"Thank you for telling me that — Jeff," she said softly.

"So I take it I won't be seeing you at my maths class on Tuesdays any longer?" he asked her, and there was no need to answer.

After a moment he said, quietly, "But I want to see you again. Can I come round, sometime, and visit you? I want to meet Sandra, and I want to see Gary at home, and — I want you and me to get to know each other better. Maybe you would invite me to come on a picnic with you?"

"Maybe we could do just that," Janet agreed, and somewhere inside her a small golden glow began to grow.

She looked at her watch.

"I'd better get home," she said a little breathlessly, knowing that he was watching her, his eyes on her face. "Gary will think I've been kept in after school."

They walked together round the corner to the school, and he took her car key from her and opened the door.

"Goodnight, Janet," he said through the window. "See you soon."

The words were simple, but she knew that he meant them. It might be tomorrow, it might be the next day, but — she knew she *would* see him soon. □

It had captured them both in its spell — two lonely people trying to forget that reality waited at the end of the cruise.

Holiday Magic

C HARLES T. FLEMING surfaced from the ultramarine depths of the liner's swimming pool. He hauled himself on to the side, enjoying the pleasant warmth of the sun-soaked tiles. He dried himself briskly, and noticed that already, after only one day out, he was sporting a noticeable if undistinguished tan.

Most of the other passengers looked as though they spent every available moment drenched in tropical sunshine. They certainly seemed to indulge in a continuous feverish ritual of oiling and sunning themselves.

He watched one girl in a trim white swimsuit as she took to the green depths in a really rather elegant dive. She came up for air half a yard from where he sat, and smiled brightly at him. "It's a lovely day, Mr Fleming. The captain says we're going to have *the* most marvellous cruise," she said.

C.T. Fleming stared blankly at the sun-tanned face and the sleek glistening hair, and his eyes took in the golden shoulders and the curvy lines of the white swimsuit. He peered closer, wishing he'd had his glasses with him.

But it was really the *voice*. The voice was definitely familiar. And as he hadn't exchanged more than two words with anyone since he'd arrived on board, it had to be someone he knew.

The girl smiled again and prepared to launch herself backwards into the pool.

"Deidre Bishop, Mr Fleming. Lingerie and housecoats."

And she was gone, cutting through the water like some graceful sea creature.

Complete Story by GRETA NELSON

HOLIDAY MAGIC

C.T. felt a surge of disappointment as recognition and realisation dawned simultaneously. Good grief, it was Miss Bishop, head of Lingerie.

What was she doing here, on his sacred, annual pilgrimage away from the store? She should be safely tucked away amongst her cami-knickers and controlling girdles.

"Blast!" he muttered to himself, and made straight for his cabin, where he stayed safely hidden until it was time for dinner.

As he dressed, he began to dread that she might have been put at his table, instead of that nice Finnish family who spoke no English and therefore didn't intrude at all on his privacy. Last night, over the delicious sole meuniere and chocolate profiteroles, they'd exchanged wide, appreciative smiles and little else.

He really couldn't bear it if his solitude were to be invaded.

He closed his eyes and thought of Deidre Bishop as he usually saw her, on his weekly round of the store. She was slim and neat and impeccably dressed, her fair hair tucked efficiently into some sort of French pleat, and her voice pleasantly unobtrusive. She'd hardly changed at all over the years.

Her department was one of the best in the whole place — there were very few internal problems in Lingerie.

Then he thought of her as he'd seen her this afternoon by the pool. What an amazing tan — it seemed an unlikely product of Fleming's indoor strip lighting. And didn't she always spend her holidays in Devon?

He finished dressing and decided not to have a drink in the bar tonight. The Finnish family was already in the dining-room, smiling and eating with an equal amount of enthusiasm. He found himself relaxing again, and enjoyed the lobster bisque.

It was during his appreciation of the boeuf-en-croute that Deidre Bishop made her entrance — and not alone. Her escorts were male, Italian and very attentive. C.T. noticed Deidre Bishop's slinky, halter-necked dress, the bare smooth shoulders, and the glittering fall of blonde hair.

She was looking up at one of the Italians as she passed C.T.'s table, and he realised his fears of her intruding upon his evening were groundless. She apparently hadn't even noticed him.

He munched steadily through the meal, now and again casting a glance towards the corner table. The Italians were paying court in extravagant style, and Miss Bishop was coping admirably. She tempered her laughter with elegance, and managed to convey a general air of composure. It was admirable.

All those years in Lingerie has done that, he thought. She'd been superb, for instance, last Christmas, during that fiasco with the local dragon, Lady Drummond Ross. A right Tartar if ever there was one, and some idiot had sold her special order to another customer.

C.T. had expected skin and fur to fly, and made his way to the department like a new soldier facing his first enemy. But all had been sweetness and light. Miss Bishop had been offering the olive branch of coffee and eclairs, with the firm promise of a repeat order within a week.

And C.T. had taken refuge in his office, grateful that yet another crisis had been avoided.

Sometimes he felt he had submerged his whole personality and inner self in the store. Had his sense of duty not been so strong and demanding, he would have dearly liked to have shaken himself free of Flemings and all it stood for.

Somewhere inside him still was the lover of literature, the would-be writer. He thought of the novels he was burning to write and smiled ruefully. Perhaps it was already too late; he would be 40 next year.

Time was the eternal enemy.

C.T. emerged from his introspection and realised that time in its more mundane guise was nudging him out of the dining-room. The waiters hovered respectfully and C.T. noticed he was the last diner to leave.

The night air was lovely, warm and sweet, with gentle little breezes coming up from the sea. The coloured lights strung across the deck were like brilliantly-lit jewels, flashing at each gentle movement.

C.T. moved to the rail and looked out over the dark mysterious ocean. He stood there for an hour or more, absorbing the calm, the beauty of it all.

He heard the music from the ballroom as he turned towards his cabin, and he wondered idly if Miss Bishop was now displaying unexpected talents on the dance floor.

He started up the next flight of steps and collided with Deidre Bishop as she came round the corner, very fast. C.T. frowned. The speed seemed to indicate what he could only describe as panic, and he glimpsed tears in the soft brown eyes.

He held her arms gently for a moment, and she looked up at him. Then she pulled away, stumbling carelessly down the iron stairway.

C.T. Fleming stared after her, then turned, to see one of the Italians standing at the top of the steps. It was the younger, better looking of the two, and he smiled blandly at C.T. He raised his shoulders in resignation.

"The English," he said. "They are unbelievable. They say one thing and mean another."

He clapped a hand to his forehead and bade C.T. a cheerful goodnight.

C.T. clenched his hands around the stair rail and stayed there until his anger subsided. He couldn't remember the last time he had so badly wanted to punch someone on the nose.

DEIDRE BISHOP lay in her cabin. Dry eyed and motionless, she stared into the darkness. The horror of tonight's humiliation, almost directly in front of C.T. Fleming, swept over her like a tidal wave, leaving her drained and hot with shame.

Had she asked for it? Wasn't the very fact of her being here at all a reflection of her uncharacteristic lack of inhibition, a deviation from the norm?

She'd known perfectly well that this was C.T.'s annual jaunt, and she had made her plans with precision.

She'd made elaborate arrangements with the local welfare officers to ensure that her mother should be well looked after, and she'd managed to persuade a distant cousin to come and live in for the whole three weeks.

She had launched into an obsessive course of physical self-improvement, attending gymnasium sessions in her lunch hour, and spending a small fortune (and a great deal of time) on an effective sun-bed in a newly-opened salon.

She had blown three months' salary on clothes for the cruise, veering for the first time in her life towards stylish, provocative garments.

In short, she was like a gambler who had decided to gather his all, in one last desperate bid.

In the darkened cabin now, Deidre Bishop moved slightly in protest against her merciless self-analysis. Surely *desperate* was too harsh a word? Surely she was only indulging in innocent day-dreams?

She was good at day-dreaming. She'd been at Flemings now for 17 years, ever since she'd left school, and for 15 of those years she'd been in love with C.T. She, alone in the whole world, was aware of her unsuitable, fruitless passion.

Occasionally, she regretted her total commitment, and wished she could start again as a fresh-faced 17-year-old, on the threshold of life, avid for adventure and experience.

Instead of which, she had taken one look at C.T. all those years ago, and her world had telescoped immediately. Several hopeful young men had asked her out over the years, and the outings were polite and friendly, but strangely detached and uncomfortable.

As time went by, the invitations became less frequent, and this suited Deidre Bishop quite well. She had chosen her obsession and was prepared for the inevitable deprivations.

So her life was divided between the neat detached house in a quiet suburb, and the Lingerie department, where she knew her work was second to none. If she secretly despaired when the girls gossiped about C.T.'s latest female admirer, she recovered quickly. She was in total control of herself. And then, three months ago, she had been having lunch with Mrs Powell, C.T.'s personal assistant.

Mrs Powell had attacked her chicken with enthusiasm, and sighed.

"Mr Fleming's off on the ocean blue as usual this year. What wouldn't I give for a cruise in the Adriatic." Mrs Powell had become more confidential. "It's not all that expensive, either. Quite a few cancellations apparently, so they've dropped the price a bit."

They moved on to the sweet course and talked of other things, but a wild, improbable seed of thought was already planted in Deidre Bishop's mind.

She couldn't, she just couldn't think of it. Surely.

On the other hand, she needed a holiday, not just their usual annual two weeks in Devon. She really needed a break, and C.T. hadn't a monopoly on luxury cruises, after all. The liner would surely be big enough for them both.

She called in at the travel agency on the way home, and the wheels were set in motion.

She lay now in the elegant cabin with its satin coverlets and thick-pile carpets, and wished with all her heart that she was at their usual hotel at Paignton. She would be giving her mother the next day's itinerary, wondering if there would be fish for lunch again the next day.

She longed for the mundane, boring routine of it all. And tomorrow and the rest of the cruise loomed large and hostile, like some doom-ridden cloud.

DEIDRE BISHOP didn't appear at breakfast, and C.T. noticed that the two Latin Romeos had already succeeded in getting a bubbly redhead in tow. He finished his marmalade and toast dispiritedly, and felt a strangely fierce disappointment for Miss Bishop.

From all he'd heard, her life was far from easy. An elderly, invalid mother at home, the routine slog at work. There had been a rumour last year that Frank Jopling from accounts was being more than attentive to her.

C.T. shifted on his chair and thought of Deidre Bishop's eyes last night, large and lost and wet with tears. Those eyes didn't belong to a girl who would go for Frank Jopling's mania for precision and organisation.

He drained his third cup of coffee and went to get ready for their

Gideon's WAY

More impressions of life
from the Highlands of Scotland, by
GIDEON SCOTT MAY,
observer of people and nature alike . . .

A HIVE OF ACTIVITY

**Gideon receives an unusual gift
— a swarm of extremely
busy bees.**

THE hills are at their magnificent best, proudly raising their heads as they wrap purple plaids around their shoulders. The bees fly higher to collect the coveted heather pollen — but how do they know where to go?

Each hive has specially-selected scouts whose job is to survey the countryside for flowers waiting, willingly, to be plundered for their pollen. When they find what they are looking for, the scouts fly straight back to the hive, where the "workers" are waiting to welcome them, gathering in a circle.

The scouts make their entrance, marching in soldierly single file to the centre of the circle. With every movement of their bodies, they begin to dance a rhythmic message and, with uncanny accuracy, convert the circle into a compass, pirouetting like Liberty horses in a circus ring, pausing to point out, in detail, the direction to be taken for today's collection of honey-making pollen.

The workers take off, wave after wave, and the high-pitched buzzing of their departure fades as they fly into the distance, directly on course!

Who was more qualified to acquaint me with the fascinating facts of the

HOLIDAY MAGIC

first trip on shore.

C.T. noticed Deidre Bishop, sitting at the far side of the embarking launch. She was wearing a cool, ice-pink dress and had tied a matching scarf over her hair. Her sunglasses were big and mysterious, hiding tell-tale signs of last night's tears, he guessed.

There was an aloofness about her today which reminded him of how she was at work — efficient and self-possessed. For as long as he could remember, she had managed to convey that sort of impression.

The passengers spilled out on to the landing pier. They were like a flock of chattering, colourful birds, C.T. thought. He glimpsed a fast-disappearing flash of pink as Deidre Bishop hailed a pony and trap. He had an absurd desire to run after her and ask if he could share her day's sightseeing.

Instead, he had a delicious coffee and cream at an open restaurant, and spent four hours seeing the local churches, standing quietly in their dark stone coolness, feeling the sense of untouched history

156

bee business than "The Beeman."

The Beeman's wife buzzed around like a queen bee herself. She had spent most of her life "in service" and it is said in the Strath that she had catered for "crowned heads" and, indeed, her cooking was fit for a king.

The Beeman's wife had a mission in life — to cook mouth-watering meals that would make people beat a path to her table. Today's lunch was steak and kidney pie. Every morsel melted in my mouth. Yum!

Like a well-fed lion, I felt like lying down somewhere, but The Beeman presented me with a spare hive containing a surplus swarm of bees. As he waved me goodbye, he said, "There's such a lot these clever creatures can teach us. I learn something new every day.

"Mind you," he added, "Geordie of the Glen is a good man with bees, but only because he suffers from rheumatism and firmly believes that their stinging will supply a cure.

"So he takes a handful of bees to bed with him every night! That's why," the Beeman continued, "he has marital problems."

I soon found out that there was a lot more to bees than watching the workers clock in and out. Having just completed my first attempt at fitting honey sections into the hive and triumphantly returning for tea, Irralee remarked about a ceaseless humming sound and tracked it down to my kilt.

A cautious peep revealed several hundred sizzling bees in every pleat. I was directed to hang my kilt on the garden fence until the bees tired of admiring the tartan.

It could have been a lot worse, I assured Irralee, and told her of how Geordie of the Glen took bees to bed with him as a cure for rheumatism, but she just treated me to a "pull the other leg" look.

I spent the following day scything thistles. In the evening, I could feel the protestations from my shoulder muscles. I mentioned this to Irralee at bedtime but she lay silently under the reading lamp, with a book cast to one side, her eyes closed.

"Maybe," I said, "it could be rheumatism. I think I'll go to the hive and get a handful of bees."

Irralee opened one eye and said slowly, "Don't you dare!"

It became crystal clear to me, at that moment, why Geordie of the Glen had marital problems. □

HOLIDAY MAGIC

seeping through him. He couldn't wait to get back to his cabin to put it all down on paper.

He was late going into dinner that night, and he passed Deidre Bishop in close consultation with the purser about a change of table. C.T. overheard the slight irritation in the purser's voice, and slowly retraced his steps. His tone and his grey eyes were equally cool.

"I imagine it won't give you too much trouble to accommodate Miss Bishop. In fact, I noticed this morning at breakfast that there is an unoccupied table by the door. Miss Bishop and I are old friends and it would suit us very well if you could arrange for us both to eat there tonight."

He smiled equably at the surprised purser.

"Meanwhile, we'll have a drink in the bar and that will give your staff ample time to see to things." And he closed his fingers round Deidre Bishop's left elbow, and propelled her into the smoky atmosphere of the bar.

They sat on high stools, sipping their drinks and he asked her about her day's sightseeing in Marallo. He watched her and enjoyed her growing relaxation as she talked.

She spoke enthusiastically about a local glass-blowing industry and promised to show him what she'd bought there.

"They really are beautiful." Her eyes were wide and luminous in the darkened bar, and C.T. Fleming felt suddenly that this was a moment to be treasured. Deidre Bishop's eyes widened further. "You don't think it might be worth importing some for the store, do you? They really are truly exquisite — I know they'd be an absolute sell-out."

C.T. held her gaze sternly. "You've just broken my golden rule. The store is a forbidden word while I'm on board ship, and dire consequences await those who break my rule."

He smiled and held up his glass. "To our cruise, Miss Bishop. May it be the best ever."

And it was perfect. C.T. couldn't remember when his enjoyment had been so total. He longed for the start of each new day and its non-stop programme of exciting, different things to do.

They visited ancient sea ports and absorbed the primitive history of the people. They swam in the hot blue lagoons and sunned themselves on deserted white beaches. They talked over dinner and C.T. even confided his desire to write.

They danced to slow romantic music in the gold and white ballroom and Deidre Bishop, held closely against C.T., sent up little prayers of thanks that this had all proved so magical.

If she occasionally felt like Cinderella, fearing that the dreaming had to stop, she didn't care. She was prepared to re-enter her own world later, knowing she'd be happy that her holiday had been so good.

But her own world claimed her sooner than she could have imagined. On the Monday of the second week, the telegram arrived to say that her mother had died, and arrangements had been made for her immediate journey home.

C.T. stood there in the sparkling golden sunshine, and he felt his world rock about him. It was as if a long-promised dream was being destroyed in an instant.

They hardly spoke again, until she came to say goodbye just as the helicopter was arriving to take her home to death and sadness.

C.T. raised a hand and touched her cheek. "I'm so very sorry." He wondered if he should offer to return with her. But already there was a barrier of convention and old habit between them.

Deidre Bishop's eyes had lost their light and she hardly seemed to see him.

Already she was engulfed with a mighty burden of guilt. If she'd been at home, instead of jet-setting on a luxury cruise, maybe her mother would still be alive. She thought briefly of the past idyllic days — it was already a dream, a forbidden glimpse of what might have been.

She turned away from C.T. and went towards the helicopter without another word.

O N his first day back at work, C.T. checked that a wreath had been sent from him personally, and he walked through the Lingerie department unusually often. The place was running with its normal efficiency, but there was no sign of Deidre Bishop.

On his fourth visit, C.T. plucked up enough courage to approach Miss Mellers.

Miss Mellers was as old as Flemings itself, and was the soul of discretion. If she felt any curiosity at Mr Fleming's intensity, she betrayed none. She told him, quietly, that Miss Bishop had asked for specially extended leave due to the circumstances.

On Friday afternoon, C.T. sat dismally through the board meeting and knew that the time had come to tell his father that a new managing director would have to be found. This entire week had been unproductive, uninspired, a constant reminder that life was slipping by. He had spent too long stifling his inner hopes and ambitions.

He thought of the notes he had made during the cruise, all that submerged creativity. Time, he thought. So much time we spend doing things we don't really care about. We're slaves to convention and duty and Time. And eventually Time runs out.

He glanced at his watch and saw that the meeting still had an hour to go. He could see the tops of the poplar trees in the park, and he watched as they moved gently in the wind. He closed his eyes and thought of Deidre Bishop on the cruise. He remembered her sensitivity, her deep appreciation of all that was beautiful.

He thought of her years of duty, her unstinting loyalty. Suddenly, very badly, he wanted to hear her soft, gentle voice, to look into the warm brown eyes, to hold her against him.

He stood up suddenly and saw the surprise on the faces of his father and the other board members. C.T.'s smile was brilliant, and as sure as it could be.

"Urgent business, gentlemen," he said and he didn't even wait to pick up his briefcase . . .

Deidre Bishop looked out at her mother's beloved rose garden.

HOLIDAY MAGIC

Her guilt had become an almost physical thing, even though she knew it had no logic, no rational base.

It was really her own punishment for the enormous sense of disappointment the telegram had evoked in her. Her despair at her mother's death — but disappointment that her golden days were over.

Her sense of shame had taken over almost immediately and she had mourned, truly, for her mother, but she couldn't let go of her self-chastisement yet.

She had already considered a change of job. With her experience, almost any of the top stores would be glad to have her, and the move would do her good.

A new beginning, a new life. She felt stronger already, full of determination.

But the next moment, her legs turned to jelly at the amazing sight of C.T. Fleming storming up the front path. His ring at the doorbell was just as peremptory — it actually sounded as though he were leaning against it.

C.T. stared down at her, and Deidre called upon a lifetime of self-control. There was a most distracting urgency about him.

"There wasn't any time to say what I wanted on board ship. There never is time, we can never count on a new day dawning. Time is our constant enemy from the day we are born."

C.T. regarded her solemnly for a moment. "I'm sorry about your mother."

He saw the shutter slam down, covering the soft brown eyes, and he went on with steady purpose. "Your mother was elderly, I believe, and an invalid. So it must have been the right time for her to die — you couldn't have wanted anything else for her."

He saw the anger fighting with the guilt, and was glad that the anger won. It came out in a fury of tears and bitter, stinging words. He quietly stepped inside the door and held her against him until the storm of sobbing had worn itself out.

"That's better," he said and turned her face up to his. "That's much better." His kiss was gentle and deliberate. Deidre Bishop closed her eyes and leaned against him for a moment, then stiffened.

"I'm thinking of leaving the store," she said.

C.T. leaned against the door frame and looked down at her.

"Good," he said. "I hoped you might. A budding novelist needs a wife to sharpen pencils, and provide coffee and comforts."

He saw the apprehension in Deidre Bishop's eyes, and he wished he could eliminate all the uncertainty, instantly and for ever. But for the moment he was grateful for the small flicker of hope inside him, giving him courage and strength.

And to celebrate, he kissed her again. □

© Greta Nelson 1981.

160

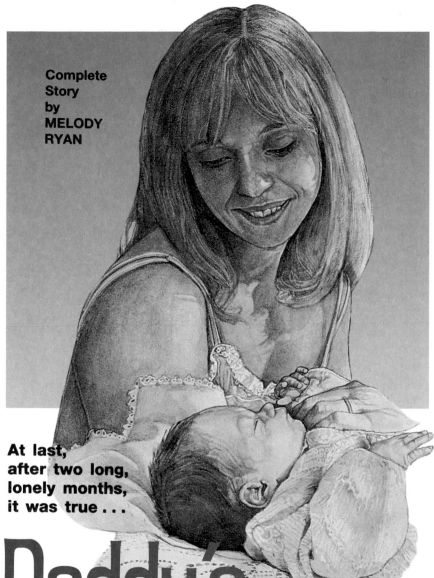

Complete
Story
by
MELODY
RYAN

At last,
after two long,
lonely months,
it was true . . .

"Daddy's Coming Home"

"DADDY'S COMING HOME"

SITTING curled up on the sofa, Katie flicked through a magazine without interest. She felt restless and nervous, and her heart beat faster every time she heard the sound of an approaching car.

Her eyes were forever darting to the clock.

As if in response, the painted cuckoo burst from the wooden clock on the wall, noisily proclaiming eight o'clock.

She stood up and went across to the window. Looking out at the cold night and glinting stars, her heart beat painfully as she thought of the aeroplane, flying through the darkness, down towards the lights of the airport.

Even now, the taxi could be on its way . . .

Upstairs, the baby began crying. Katie went up at once, bending to lift up the tiny form and cradling it against her.

It was so strange, she thought, her lips pressed against the wispy hair, so strange that she should have produced such a beautiful, fragile creature. Two months ago there had been nothing but her and an empty house, and something unknown and unseen, kicking boldly as it grew inside her.

It had been hard when Derek went away. Hard for him, too, for he had not wanted to leave her, so near the birth of their child. But it had been a marvellous opportunity for him to go out to the Middle East, and she had persuaded him to go.

And now the waiting was over, and soon he would be home. Yet somewhere, beneath her excitement and her joy, she was worried.

She cuddled her child, whispering softly into the darkness.

"There, Charlotte, sleep now. Go to sleep. And when you wake you will see your daddy. He will be here soon. Daddy's coming home . . ."

She heard a car drawing up, followed by footsteps on the path. The doorbell sounded through the tiny house.

In the sitting-room, Derek held her at arm's length, and stared for a long time into her face.

"Are you all right, Katie?"

"Yes. Yes, I'm fine."

"Are you sure?" He studied her anxiously. "You look pale."

She laughed. "That's only because you're so used to sun-tanned faces! I'm OK. Really! And I can see you're well. You look fantastic!"

He smiled at her. And she stood, watching him while she waited for him to ask.

Eventually he said, quietly and shyly, "And — the baby? How is she?"

"Fine. Just fine. Come and see her."

He followed her upstairs, and into Charlotte's room.

"She — she's like you, isn't she?" Derek said. And Katie smiled.

But in her heart she said: *She's not a bit like me. She's not like anyone in particular. But you don't know what else to say, do you?*

Because she sensed his awkwardness, she switched off the light, and said gently, "Come on. You can see her properly in the morning."

Derek relaxed on the sofa while she made coffee. She sat cross-legged on the rug while they sipped their drinks and talked about the previous weeks.

Or rather, she listened while he talked of his experiences.

Yet how would she share with him those things that had happened to her? The loneliness and fear, the hospital bed, the tears and the pain, and the joy which washed it all away?

She sighed, not knowing where to begin. In the end she said nothing — just listened while Derek spoke.

He spoke long into the night, until suddenly he noticed her stifled yawn.

"You must be tired," he said gently. "Sorry, I wasn't thinking."

She smiled, wondering if he knew what tiredness really was. Total exhaustion at the end of each day, falling into bed and yearning for sleep — a sleep which could not come, because if it came it might swallow her completely, then who would hear if the baby started crying?

She stood up, smoothing the creases from her dress. Then while Derek prepared for bed, she washed the cups and set the breakfast table.

Why didn't he touch their baby? Why didn't he want to pick her up and cuddle her?

The worry which had been nagging at Katie all evening, all day, and for days before that, grew a little larger.

B Y the time she climbed into bed he was asleep. She curled up beside him, listening to his regular breathing, and trying to remember all the things he'd told her.

She wanted to know about those two missing months: to her, they were as important as all the other months in the three years they had shared together. Suddenly she realised there were tears running down her cheeks . . .

In the silence of the early hours, she awoke. In her dreams she heard a baby crying.

Stretching, she turned over — and found that the space next to her was empty. Anxious, she sat up, and headed towards the baby's room.

At the door she stopped, confused and amazed. Unaware of her watching, Derek sat awkwardly cradling the baby. Gently he rocked her to sleep, a frown of concentration on his face.

"There now," he whispered to the drowsy child. "Everything's all right now. Daddy's home."

Katie stared at her daughter, then at her husband — and she smiled. She recognised in his face the beginnings of something she, too, had known: the slow dawning of a kind of wonder . . . □

MANDY LAWSON, at seven years old, was very content with her life. Every morning when her mother took her to school in her small blue car, they sang songs, sometimes quietly in time with the engine sounds, sometimes more loudly.

Every evening, Grandad met her from his office and they went home on the Underground. Sometimes Grandad hardly spoke, but he had a twinkle in his eyes that was only dulled when his ulcer was very bad.

And he rarely stopped Mandy from going down on the up escalator, and up on the down one.

Mandy had lived with her mother and grandad since her father died.

Take one small girl, some ordinary people, a lot of imagination, and there you have the beginning of a real, honest-to-goodness fairy tale . . .

Once Upon A Time

Complete Story by SUSAN SALLIS

Then there was school: school was all right, especially singing, play-time and story-time. Mr Bates told lovely stories. He never used a book and drew on the blackboard as he spoke. So his stories came to life.

There were always castles, dungeons, princes and princesses in the stories and Mandy often thought that the princesses looked very like her mother.

One day Simon Ellerway said, "Why don't you tell us about real things, sir?"

Mr Bates looked amazed. "But I do, Simon," he said. "If you look around you, you'll always see a princess being rescued from a dragon by a prince. Those are real things."

Simon Ellerway was puzzled. "I wanna hear about spaceships and robots, and terrible creatures from outer space," he announced.

Jenny Gibbons sneered. "That's not real, Simon Ellerway. That's invented."

Mr Bates frowned. "I'm not so sure, Jenny. I think, for Simon, spaceships are as real as princesses are for me."

He looked rather apologetic. "It's just that I don't know enough about space to tell those stories. How would it be if Simon told you a space story tomorrow and I tried to do the drawings?"

Mandy put up her hand. "Sir, the day after that, can I tell a story? And you do the drawings?"

"Certainly, Mandy. What will your story be about?"

Mandy thought carefully. "I don't know yet, sir. But it'll be real — like yours. And like Simon's."

"Wonderful. Marvellous." Mr Bates smiled.

That day at three-thirty, Grandad came to take her home as usual. He stood just inside the playground, apart from the mothers and pushchairs, reading his newspaper. With his rolled umbrella hooked over one arm, and his bowler hat tipped forbiddingly over his eyes, no-one would have dared speak to him.

Grandad always rolled his newspaper up as Mandy approached, tapped her once on top of the head, then turned and marched down the road towards the Underground. She always fell into step beside him, and depending upon his ulcer, sometimes they talked, sometimes they didn't.

They understood each other very well, and if he grunted once more than usual Mandy would ask sympathetically, "Is it your tummy?"

He would grunt again and she would stop talking and have an interesting think until they reached home.

Today he grunted a lot, so Mandy decided to think about her story.

She stood beneath his newspaper on the way down the escalator, and thought it could be a tent and she might tell a story about Red Indians.

As they waited for the arrival of their train, Grandad said

grumpily, "Like moles. That's what we are — moles burrowing away underground every single day!"

Mandy thought she might tell the class a story about being a real live mole.

But she knew she really wanted to tell a story like the ones Mr Bates told. A story full of beauty, adventure, bravery, love and danger. Maybe that was happening right now! Perhaps she had better have a look.

There was only one person who could have been a princess in the compartment. She had long blonde hair, blue eyes, and she carried a rolled-up magazine in such a way that it could possibly have been a wand in disguise. Unfortunately, she also wore jeans and a scruffy old cardigan over her T-shirt.

Mandy looked round surreptitiously for a prince. Sitting next to the princess was a fairly likely-looking man. But farther along the compartment was someone Mandy considered to be far more suitable.

Yes, this prince wore a very smart suit and his hair was combed, but still wavy. He reminded Mandy of Mr Bates.

Next to him there was yet another man. Mandy didn't like his beard, nor his glasses, and his jeans were almost falling apart. He wouldn't really do — unless he was in disguise, of course.

She pulled one of her bunches of hair forward and sucked the end consideringly.

Grandad could obviously see right through his newspaper because he immediately tapped her head.

"Don't suck your hair," he commanded.

She stopped sucking and looked at all the people in her story. The princess was still gazing into space, obviously waiting to be rescued.

None of the princes were even looking at her, but the man at the end, with the beard and glasses, suddenly looked up from his magazine, caught Mandy's eyes, and grinned.

Maybe he had been told off for sucking his moustache at some time or other, Mandy thought.

AFTER tea, Mandy sat cross-legged on the rug and explained her problem. Mother entered into the discussion wholeheartedly.

"It can't very well be the one sitting next to the princess," she said, pausing in her knitting. "Because, you see, darling, there has to be something keeping them apart. If not an actual dragon then perhaps — "

"You're as potty as the child!" Grandad snorted. "No wonder I've got an ulcer!"

"There were two ladies between the princess and the Mr Bates-prince," Mandy said, thoughtfully. "And one of them looked very fierce."

Mother looked up quickly at the mention of Mr Bates' name, then she put down her knitting and clasped her hands.

"I wouldn't be a bit surprised if the fierce lady is the princess's wicked stepmother. She's forbidden the prince to speak to the princess, so every afternoon she goes and sits there between them!"

"That's enough of that, Kate. Between you and that schoolmaster, Mandy won't know fact from fancy." Grandad snorted.

"Mr Bates is the best schoolmaster in the world," Mandy said, definitely. "And when he draws his princesses, they look just like you, Mummy."

Mother's fair skin turned pink. "Really?" she said, carelessly. "I must admit Mr Bates made a good impression on me at the last open day."

The next day, Simon Ellerway told a story about an unidentified flying object that landed in his back yard and took away his older, bossy sister.

"You only said that because you don't like your sister," Jenny Gibbons commented.

Simon Ellerway droned on. "And then the thing from outer space reached over the fence, lifted up Jenny Gibbons, too, and went away, never to be seen again."

Jenny Gibbons said accusingly, "That's no story. It hasn't got an ending."

"That's the ending," Simon said, inexorably.

Jenny had an edge of panic in her voice. "Well, I don't like it. It's not a happy ending, and it didn't last long enough."

"I think it might be the beginning of a serial, don't you, Simon?" Mr Bates suggested. "We could call it 'Adventures In Outer Space', and perhaps the next time you could set off to rescue Jenny and your sister."

"Why?" Simon asked baldly.

"Because it will make an exciting story," Mr Bates said, as the bell rang.

Mandy waited until everyone was in the cloakroom before she approached Mr Bates with the outline of her story.

"It sounds very good, Mandy," Mr Bates congratulated her.

"Yes, but there's no ending, sir," Mandy explained. "Not even as much ending as Simon Ellerway's story!"

"Mmm . . ." Mr Bates frowned, and chewed at his pencil.

Then he said, inexplicably, "I've been meaning to ask you, is your mother able to come to the dance in aid of the school swimming pool?"

Mandy was bewildered. "She says she's got nothing to wear. But what about my ending, sir?"

"I was thinking of my ending," Mr Bates said. "Tell her to wear anything — anything at all." He smiled suddenly. "What we need, Mandy, is a magic spell."

Mandy nodded eagerly, confused, but grateful that he had been listening after all. "That's smashing, sir. But what good would that do?"

Mr Bates looked thoughtful. "A spell to make the princess realise that she's got a prince right under her nose!"

Mandy nodded again. "Yes, sir. Go on, sir."

"Well, that's the problem, isn't it? I've been trying to think of one for ages."

Mandy sighed. Mr Bates didn't seem to be quite himself today. Grandad was her only hope.

Grandad was reading his paper with enormous concentration as Mandy came across the playground. "Grandad, I've got something very important to ask you. You must answer, please, even if your ulcer is really bad."

Grandad folded his paper and tapped her head.

"All right, just one question and one answer."

Mandy said, "Well, all I want to know is . . . what's a magic spell to wake up a princess and make her look at her prince and — and — give him a kiss?"

Grandad looked into the distance. "That's obvious, my girl, and as soon as any woman hears it she looks around for her man. And unless he's pretty nippy on his feet, she generally manages to catch him."

"What *is* it, Grandad?"

" 'The Wedding March'!" Grandad said, and stumped down the street towards the Underground.

Mandy sighed. She had the feeling that Grandad had made one of his little jokes that she rarely understood.

MANDY and Grandad had to stand on the train. Grandad hung on to his strap with one hand and held his paper with the other.

Mandy could hardly believe her luck. The princess was there again, staring into space, flanked on one side by one of the princes and on the other by the same straight-faced lady who was obviously a dragon.

Two or three seats farther down was the prince who looked like Mr Bates. Unfortunately, he was asleep today. But the prince with the beard and the glasses was awake.

Mandy looked at them one by one. She realised that though there were three princes, only one of them would recognise the magic spell and be brave enough to leap past the dragon and claim his lady.

Then, as they drew away from Bond Street, the noise died and they came to a standstill. Mandy looked along the line of faces. Nobody else took any notice of the sudden eerie stillness — they were quite used to delays. It was only Mandy Lawson who knew this delay was for a very special purpose indeed.

She jabbed at Grandad's paper to warn him, then said loudly, "Now is the time!"

Everyone looked startled. Grandad rustled his paper irritably.

The first prince said, "What's going on, then?"

The dragon smiled at Mandy and said softly, "Don't worry, dear, it's all right."

Mandy knew that was simply intended to throw her off her guard. She looked down at Prince-Mr Bates, and repeated more loudly, "Now is the *time*!"

Prince-Mr Bates woke up, and stared at her. The bearded prince shoved his magazine into his bag and leaned forward.

"Now is the time for what?" he asked with interest.

Mandy said commandingly, "Time for the spell! Listen!" And she began to sing. "Tum, tum-ti-tum . . . Tum tum-ti-tum . . . Tum, tum-ti-tum, tum, tum tum-ti-ti tum-ti-tum . . ."

The effect of this was certainly magical. The princess jumped to her feet as if she'd been stung. She looked wildly down the carriage at the bearded prince.

"I suppose you arranged this!" she said angrily. "Not content with following me night after night, you have told this innocent child to —"

The bearded prince also leaped to his feet. He was spluttering with laughter.

"Darling, honestly, I don't know this little girl from Adam — or rather Eve! But don't you see, it's all meant to be. Like a fairy story."

The first prince repeated like a parrot, "What's going on, then? Has some joker pulled the emergency lever? I've got an urgent appointment."

Grandad said grimly, "It's no wonder I've got an ulcer!"

"It's a dream. I'm still asleep," Prince-Mr Bates said.

The dragon said in a reasonable voice, "Now, just a moment. There's no need to panic."

And Mandy shouted, "Take no notice of her! She's a dragon in disguise! Just listen to the magic spell! Tum tum-ti-tum . . . tum tum-ti-tum . . .''

"Madam, I apologise most humbly. My granddaughter is a little . . . a little . . ." Mandy's grandad, for once, was completely lost for words.

"A little darling," the bearded prince murmured as he hugged the princess.

"A little potty," Grandad said firmly. He sat in the seat vacated by the princess, and began to talk to the dragon. The train began moving again.

The princess sat on the lap of the bearded prince, and the other two princes relapsed into an embarrassed silence.

Mandy stayed where she was. Not only did she have the ending to her story, but it seemed as if she had the beginning of another one. One about the dragon and the elderly knight.

ONE week later, Kate Lawson attended the dance in aid of the school swimming pool. She wore a long velvet skirt, and a white blouse.

At last, Mr Bates held Kate in his arms. He waltzed her sedately around the room.

"Mandy is doing well with her stories, Mrs Lawson," he said. "We had a third one today."

"Really?" Kate was surprised. "I know about the princess, and there is one about an elderly knight slaying a dragon —"

"Today's was about a queen who ruled her nation very well but wanted someone who could help her. She's looking everywhere, but as there's a special qualification, it's proving to be rather a difficult task."

"What's the special qualification?" Kate asked.

"Well, it has to be someone with magical powers, just like herself."

"Oh dear. What kind of magical powers does she have?"

"She can make everything, even quite ordinary things, into exciting adventures. She has magical laughter inside herself."

Kate was silent as they circled the floor. Then she cleared her throat and asked, "And where has she found this prince with magical powers?"

Mr Bates smiled down at her. "It's a serial. I think she's going to be looking for one or two more episodes. And then, I think she'll realise she's found him."

"What if he doesn't want to take on this nation of hers? It sounds a tricky sort of a job."

Mr Bates held her more closely and smiled into her eyes.

"He'll consider it an honour, a joy and what's more great fun," he said.

And he doubled his pace and whirled her around the room while they both laughed. □

AT breakfast, Amy said, "I thought I'd invite Kathy and George for dinner on Sunday."

"Fine." Joe looked up. "When is that guy going to pop the question, anyway? They've been seeing each other for years."

"You may well ask." Amy's snub-nosed face was glum. "But he might be on the verge. Kathy told me that he noticed last week that his hair was thinning. She thought it was a hopeful sign.

"She says that maybe he'll begin to realise that he'd better start having a wife and children before it's too late."

"Hmmmm. She may have a point there." Joe reached for the marmalade. "Ah well, not every man leaps into wedlock, as I did at twenty-four. I was the reckless, impetuous type."

"Oh, some impetuous — eight months. And some proposal — right there in the street in heavy traffic. It sounded as if you were considering a merger with another company."

"You know I'm not good with words." His voice rose. "Action, not words, my girl! That's my motto! Have I not been a devoted

Complete Story by
FLORENCE JANE SOMAN

HAPPY FAMILIES

. . . was the name of the game.
Mother played it perfectly —
but Dad didn't know the rules!

and faithful husband and father these past seven years?"

"You're wonderful." Amy meant it. She loved Joe as deeply as he did her. Yet it was true that words were not his speciality. Emotional ones stuck in his throat, and compliments were rare.

Sometimes she imagined him murmuring, "You're my world" or "You're the beat of my heart." But if ever he actually said such things she would take his temperature!

Now her thoughts went to the dinner ahead. The Extra-Push Dinner, she called it, and the push was aimed at the back of the unsuspecting George.

The idea had been inspired by Kathy's wistful words: "All his friends seem to be unattached or separated or divided. If only he could see a whole, happy marriage like yours and Joe's! It might give him that little extra push!"

We'll give it a try, Amy thought. It can't hurt.

That Sunday evening, awaiting her guests, she gazed around the living-room. Joe, casually dressed and innocent as to the evening's purpose, was reading. Five-year-old Stevie was already in his pyjamas, absorbed in placing toy animals in a miniature barn. Over the comfortable clutter hung the aroma of her best beef stew.

An hour later all was going extremely well. The room radiated cheer, Joe was in a fine mood, and young Stevie was at his endearing best. Kathy's face was bright.

But it all seemed to go wrong when Amy returned to the room after putting Stevie to bed.

Joe, grinning, was saying, "You should hear Stevie's non-stop Dracula laugh — it could shatter light bulbs." Suddenly his face sobered. "But he gave us a real scare last week. He choked on some corn and practically turned blue."

Joe shook his head. "Kids! They can take twenty years off a man's life."

Amy cut in quickly. "Joe! Why, Stevie is a joy!"

"Remind me of that the next rainy Sunday."

It was even worse during dinner. "Just bringing up a kid today," Joe mused, "could put you in debt until you're eighty."

Amy glanced at Kathy's bleak face. Then she turned desperately to George, managing a smile. "Next month," she said, "Joe and I will have been married seven years. It seems like two!"

She gave Joe a soft, winning look, praying that he would give her one back. His answer now, she realised, wasn't just for Kathy, but for herself, too.

It was at this moment that Joe delivered the *coup de grace* to the Extra-Push Dinner.

"They say the first seven years are the hardest," he announced cheerfully. "Most divorces develop at the end of seven years."

Amy sagged back in her chair.

After dinner, Joe took George to the cellar to see his workshop. Not long after that, the two guests left, with Kathy's step leaden